Teresa Schaeffer is a novelist, screenwriter and film producer who currently resides in Boston, Massachusetts. Her most recent film project, Jack on the Rocks, is coming in the fall/winter of 2012 and other film projects are in the works.

A Forgotten Tomorrow is her second book in the Cutting Edge series. Her first work with Ransom Publishing was The Questions Within. A Forgotten Tomorrow marks her fourth published work.

IN THE SAME SERIES

A Forgotten Tomorrow

TERESA SCHAEFFER

A Forgotten Tomorrow

TERESA SCHAEFFER

Series Editor: Peter Lancett

Published by Ransom Publishing Ltd.
Radley House, 8 St. Cross Road, Winchester, Hampshire, SO23 9HX, UK
www.ransom.co.uk

ISBN 978 184167 882 5

First published in 2011
Copyright © 2011 Teresa Schaeffer
Front cover photograph: © clearviewimages

CHAPTER 1

It's funny how life can change at any moment. Two days ago I was doing my usual routine on the corner of Benz Street for my nightly work. The weather was below freezing but I still had on my old skirt, sleeveless top and hand-me-down pumps. My hair was tied up with a rubber band; my face caked with cheap make-up – days old really, since I rarely have a moment to take a shower.

Today is completely different, almost overwhelmingly different. I find myself feeling a tad uneasy while sitting here looking at the cold, white walls of Jonah's office at the City Community Center. I feel like I am in an institution being observed for some unknown mental disorder. Actually, I'm not even sure why I am here. It's stupid. He thinks that he can help me. Help me with what? I have no idea. I think I'm doing okay on my own.

Jonah found me on the corner of Benz Street a few nights ago. Benz Street is where all the girls like me hang out during the witching hour. It's the best time to get business, and without business I would never be able to survive out here.

What's my job? Well, it's obvious if anyone takes a look at my clothing. I have worn this same outfit for an entire year, except for the times I am able to get it washed. My skirt is full of holes and my top is practically falling apart – but with what I do, clothes don't really matter. It's more my attitude and sex appeal that grabs the attention of approaching men.

I am not proud of what I do, but I have to make money somewhere. I was once at the point of starvation out here, trying to live the right way. But the right way didn't turn out so well for me. Where else could I work at sixteen years old and make the money I do now? Not many places, I'd imagine. I mean, it's not great... but it is enough to get by.

I also have a slight problem with meth. It's not a bad problem really. I don't think I'm addicted completely either, I just use it every day to calm me down. Who wouldn't want to calm their nerves after nights like I have had? I don't care either. I mean, I know I can stop whenever I want to.

Anyway, back to Jonah. He thinks he can help me. What's he going to do, rent me an apartment or send me back to school? Probably not. I will let him talk, but I doubt I will have much to say.

Once he comes back into the room and sits himself at the desk, all I can do is stare. He seems to be a happy person; his eyes are smiling even when he isn't. I can't understand that either, considering he works at this place. I would picture him as being a law enforcement agent of some sort, with his thick body build and muscular arms – not a counsellor.

He sits there for a few moments before making eye contact with me again. I have no idea what this guy wants me to say or do, and it only makes me feel even more awkward when he takes out his ballpoint pen and holds it over his notebook. Again, I feel like I am being studied, but I should not be so negative. I can't help it, though.

Minutes pass as he rambles on about his program for kids like me. His goal is to take kids off the street and give them a new beginning. That's all well and good, but I'm not comfortable telling him what he wants to know – about the real me and where I came from. I'm not promising to let him help me, but I will tell him, I know I will. Even though it's not any of his business. I mean, sometimes it's good to get things out, right?

Where do I start? I don't know what I'd count as the beginning. I guess it started with my mama – if that's what you want to call her. I can't remember everything perfectly, but I will try my best.

My mama gave birth to me when she was in her early forties. I haven't seen her since I was close to nine years old. At times, I struggle to remember what she looks like, although I do remember her long, uncombed hair and how she always reeked of booze. She was rarely dressed either, unless she was working. She would lie around in her nightgown all day long.

Looking back I realise that she probably never really wanted kids – well, a kid like me at any rate. Even when I was very young, she never wanted anything to do with me. She would never play with me, help me with homework or even talk to me. The only time she spoke to me was when she wanted me to do something for her. Back then I thought it was normal for her to act like that, but now I realise that it was far from normal.

All in all I guess my early years as a child weren't too bad though. I didn't have much, but I didn't know any different, so wealth or things didn't matter. I was used to my mama being broke all the time.

Things could have been a little different if my crazy step-father Johnny had worked – he was more than capable. Now and again he did odd jobs, but never enough to help take care of a family. That was the problem I guess; he didn't see me as family. My mama didn't make him work or do anything either, probably hoping to keep him around. So he did very little around the house. He mostly obsessed about his baby – his motorcycle – or anything to do with guns and hunting.

Johnny lived with us for about a year before I was taken from my home. From when he first moved in I didn't get a chance to grow attached to him. I did the exact opposite – I tried my best to stay away.

He was a scary-looking man, about fifty years old with long, greasy hair. His intense brown eyes were likely to scare anyone who came across him in a dark alleyway. Johnny didn't talk much either – unless it was to one of his buddies who were constantly hanging around the house.

His friends were just like him, jobless and scary. I hated it when they came over because they would take over the entire house, drinking beer and smoking up the place with their disgusting cigarettes.

Well, my mama did work. In retail. But only a few days a week. She never cooked; she would stock up on all the frozen dinners she could, and that is what we ate every night. Everything else I had to do by myself. Like I said, she always smelled like booze and boozing was all she seemed to be capable of – especially after Johnny came on the scene. So, most days she remained on the couch with a cold beer in hand, drunkenly laughing at ridiculous soap operas that had no real meaning.

Again, this is how I see it now, this is what I remember. Who knows, I could be wrong – but that is all I remember about my mama.

When it came to me going to school, I did have a few problems, no matter how friendly I tried to be. I was the yucky girl who no one wanted to be friends with. My white sneakers were brown from wearing them every day, and most of my outfits were too small. Half the time I went to school wearing dirty clothes because I forgot to wash them. Eight years old and remembering to do laundry? Give me a break.

I liked going to school, though. It was my escape from everything else in my life. I still really like reading and literature, and reading was certainly a big part of my life back then. I read stories that made me happy, that took me far away from nasty Johnny or my drunken mother. I often imagined myself as the main character, reaching excellence and having a life full of love and adventure.

Johnny teased me often, as if he were a little child. Dealing with that wasn't so horrible. I just sucked it up and avoided him as much as I could. For some reason he loved to scare me in front of his friends, taunting me and telling me that ghosts were going to get me in middle of the night. The first few times I didn't take too much notice, but eventually I hated it. It didn't do any good to tell my mama. She never yelled at him about anything at all, it was always me who was scolded. And I rarely did anything wrong back then.

Anyway, eight years old was such a long time ago for me. I have blocked it out of my mind for so many years, pushing it deep down inside myself, hoping it would never surface again. I will try to explain that day as it really was, but I can't promise it will be exact.

It was in the spring, a few months before my ninth birthday. My neighbourhood was pretty small and reasonably safe. I would ride around on my bike for hours, trying to do tricks or play some sort of imaginary game. Most of the time I ended up on the ground with a scraped knee or elbow, but I didn't care. I didn't realise that day would be my last on a bike.

Johnny and his friends were in the wooded back yard of my house messing around with a pellet gun. He really shouldn't have had that thing, because he would shoot squirrels or rabbits for fun. It didn't ever kill them, but it hurt them enough that they would never be the same again. They would laugh hysterically as a squirrel struggled to crawl away after it was shot. I don't know why, but I guess it amused them.

I always played alone, so when Johnny asked me to come out back to see what he was making, I couldn't help being curious. I don't know why I allowed myself to get excited, because deep down I should have known something weird was going on. Anyway, he wouldn't tell me what it was at first, but he did give me a hint – saying it was some kind of fort for me to play in.

I don't think I ever rode my bike as fast as I did that day. I'd wanted a tree house for the longest time, but never got one. It didn't occur to me to wonder why Johnny was suddenly making one. If only I'd thought more carefully, maybe things would have turned out differently.

Big lie. When I reached them, my excitement turned to fear. Johnny and his buddies were leaning against the broken down wooden fence with odd expressions on their faces. He was holding something behind his back, but I couldn't see what it was until I got closer.

"Come here, Savannah. I got somethin' for ya," he said, in a creepy voice.

I didn't move from where I was standing. I was only a few feet away from them, but I couldn't move. It was like my legs were nailed to the ground – no matter how hard I tried, my feet wouldn't budge.

Johnny slowly walked towards me with his hands behind his back, smiling and giggling when he made eye contact with his friends. When he got close enough he showed me a half-dead squirrel that he was holding.

"See this?" he asked. "This will be you if you don't do what I tell you to."

The expression in his eyes sent chills down my spine. Suddenly I was too scared to do anything. All I could do was look at him and the poor squirrel.

"You understand me?"

I didn't say a word, just nodded my head. My hands were shaking, I felt sick to my stomach and I wanted to cry.

He took me. He took me into the shaded part of the backyard where no one would see what he was going to do. Nobody except his friends, who laughed softly as tears fell from my eyes.

That day he touched me in a place that no one had ever touched me before. I knew it wasn't right; I was terrified. All I could think about was the squirrel. If he could harm animals like he did, so swiftly and easily without a thought, what would he do to me if I told anyone? I do believe he would've killed me.

Months went by before I said anything. I would sit alone in my room all day. The visions of his evil smile that day haunted my every thought. I could still see it and I could still smell his rotten breath.

A vision came to me one day at school, making my teacher panic. We were in the middle of a maths lesson when I spaced out. Before I could stop it, my hands were clutched to my desk and tears began to fall, too quickly for me to push them back where they belonged. With that, I had the attention of the entire class, including my horrified teacher.

I didn't realise what was happening until a couple of minutes passed, and when I snapped out of it everyone was staring at me. My teacher was tapping on the desk in front of me repeatedly, asking if I was okay.

It was then that I had to... I had to tell her.

I didn't want that to happen for fear that I'd end up dead, but it took only two days before a county social worker came to my house for a visit. Johnny wasn't around when the nice lady came, only my mama and I. And boy, did Mama get angry. She yelled at me up and down, calling me a liar.

The nice lady listened to my mama rant on about how much trouble I caused and how much I lied, before taking me aside and talking with me alone. I was glad she did that too, because I wasn't lying and it wasn't fair of my mama to talk about her own daughter that way. Even at that age I knew it was wrong.

To make a long story short, I was taken from my mama that day, and haven't seen her since. It only took ten minutes of me talking to the social worker for her to realise how my life was. Of course I told her the details of what happened that day too, but by then she'd already made her decision. I don't know what I'd expected to happen. I hadn't really thought that far, and I guess further meetings with my mama must have gone on after that day. But I never knew anything about it.

CHAPTER 2

It almost makes me sick as Jonah looks at me with such a compassionate gaze upon his face. Is he serious, or is he just forcing his emotions for appeal? Either way, I wish he'd say something. If he doesn't, I will walk out of here and never look back.

There is silence for probably only a minute, but it feels like forever. Jonah looks down at his paper, writes something down and then again looks up at me with the same compassionate gaze. It's starting to annoy me.

"Sounds like your life started off pretty rough, Savannah," he says to me.

He obviously wants some kind of answer from me, but what kind of dumb remark is that? After what I just told him, of course it was a little rough. Is he an idiot?

He shifts in his chair and places his hands on top of his desk, leaning in closer to me.

"I really believe I can help you, if you will let me. We have many programs here depending on individual needs, but I have to get something back from you. You have to want this. You have to trust that I want the best outcome for you."

I stare at him for a minute before responding. I feel fidgety and anxious, and can't calm myself. This particular feeling hits me once in a while, where I want to crawl out of my skin. It's uncomfortable, but normally the anxiety subsides after a few moments if I concentrate hard enough.

"What are you gonna do for me?" I ask, with a tone that I'm sure he has heard before. I can't help but feel irritated. But I can't seem to make myself leave yet, either.

"Well," he says, "We really need to meet up again at least once or twice in my office before I can do anything."

He flips through a few papers on his desk. "My week is pretty open right now, so what do you say about maybe tomorrow, and the day following?"

"I don't understand why I have to come in here again. I told you what you wanted to know."

"I would like to know a little more about you, is all," he says with a smile. "I will talk to my partner in the meantime to see what we can do, okay? How do you feel about that? There are a lot of options and we can explore those, but sometimes just getting your thoughts out is helpful too."

"I don't know."

"It's your choice to come back here, by no means are you obligated to. You have to be the one who wants some help, I can't make you – do you understand what I mean?"

I nod my head, then immediately get out of my chair. He has been wasting my time, this guy. He is still sitting there looking at me, waiting for me to say I'm coming back. I need to leave right now, and I really need a cigarette.

"So maybe I will see you," he says to me as I walk out of the door. I keep walking, giving him no response. I don't know what I'm going to do.

I left Jonah's way too late. It's getting close to 7pm, and it's already dark. I really shouldn't have gone, because now I don't have much time to do what I need to do before shuffling off to work. Yes, work. It still is – even though it may not appeal to the general public – work.

I've come to love it here — lying underneath the run-down bridge across from Flannigan's Pub. Late at night there is an eerie silence away from centre city, the only noise being the horns blowing from the departing container ships on their journey into the dark, endless ocean. Occasionally, sirens blare quickly as they pass the deserted, forgotten area of the city. But this area is never chaotic.

Often enough it seems as if I am the only person who hangs out around this section of town, my only companions being the few stray dogs that come and feed off of Flannigan's newly discarded garbage. Once in a while a drunk from the pub wanders around aimlessly, but even that is a rarity. I like it that way though, underneath the bridge, covered by my worn and tattered blanket, looking up at the moonlit sky — alone.

I guess it gives me a lot of time to think. Sometimes thinking can be a good thing, but often enough it's not. I try to rest a little here, to ease my mind. Once I take in my happy drug of choice, I tend only to have good thoughts, and that is all I need right now.

Lately I have been a little depressed, though – without Elijah. He was my best friend, the only one I could count on out here. The only one I could count on *ever*, for that matter. It has only been two weeks since he was killed, but it feels like an eternity.

He was a boy who thought he was a man, and he had a dream. Elijah may have lived at home with his daddy, but for whatever reason he wanted to be out here on the streets. I could never understand why he wanted to leave the comfort of a warm bed, or the chance to be an educated guy behind. He just didn't care about that. He craved the buzz of life on the edge – the dealing, the power, the thrill of a city's dark secrets. All he talked about was working alongside Big Jon and his gang, supplying the city with a choice of narcotics. His drive to do this was obviously money – and lots of it. He probably watched Friday or other gang-related movies way too much. Truth is, the movies don't give the streets any justice. There is no glamour and people die way before their time. Why? Well, probably because they want to live that dream, with lots of money and fast cars. Sure, maybe they get those luxuries after a short period of time, but they might check out just as soon as they get them. I think Elijah thought it was easy – just like in the movies. How mistaken he was.

And what a mistake to think doing deals for Big Jon was the way to go. Big Jon is a well-known drug dealer and gunrunner in the city. He makes his mission look easy and justifiable, as he drives around in his loaded Escalade with one hundred dollar bills practically pouring out of his pocket. He is a big guy, probably weighing about two hundred pounds – but he always looks smart. He is never seen wearing anything other than designer clothing and expensive diamond jewellery. Many kids in this area that know of Jon idolise him for that reason alone. I would say that he probably has five or six people working for him, selling meth and cocaine to whoever will buy it. The gun-running, however, is his main source of income and he is good at it. He makes sure of it – working at night and all alone. No one in their right mind would cross his path in the wrong way because surely there would be trouble. Elijah's next goal after doing some dealing was to work alongside Jon personally, selling illegal weapons and ammo.

Well, Elijah didn't get that far, but I can't think about that right now – it only brings a deep sadness that I can't budge. So instead, before I go to work, I need a fix.

It may be sad, but meth is the only thing right now that helps. It helps me get out of this misery, this hell-hole that I call my life. Sometimes I feel incredibly lonely – alone and unwanted. It feels like I am the one who everyone directs their anger or hatred against. Am I really that horrible? Is that why I never had a family to love me? Damn, I can't keep thinking – it's driving me insane.

The thing that worries me is that I only have one bag left now from what Elijah gave me. Like I said, I'm not an addict. Meth gives me the most amazing feeling. I only use powder form. One or two lines do the job, and for about twenty minutes I feel incredibly relaxed, calm and happy. It's a state of bliss that is indescribable. A feeling I never managed to have, before now.

Granted, I never thought I'd be one to use. I remember thinking that all the girls on my block who used were ridiculous – and disgustingly skinny. I have probably lost about ten pounds, but I don't look that disgusting. Well, at least *I* don't think so, and apparently neither do my customers. Ten more pounds, though? Now, that might be going too far.

So I will lie here, under my blanket and enjoy this sensation for a while, then head off to work. My blanket is comfortable and warm, I love it. It also reminds me of Elijah.

My mind slowly drifts to a night, a couple of months or so ago. That night everything changed, for both me and Elijah.

It feels so real, as if it is happening all over again. But I smile...

I had been alone for most of the day, doing nothing at all, really. I went to the park and fed the doves a little bit of stale bread that I picked from Flannigan's trash, then walked the streets until dusk.

I remember being excited because I was going to see Elijah later on. That was something I never really felt with him before. We were best friends, and we liked to hang out together, but this really was something new.

He didn't make definite plans to come see me before I went to work, but I knew that he would. It was becoming a habit and I knew he would want to get out of his house for a while.

Anyway, I was sitting alone under my bridge for a couple of hours before I heard footsteps and the shuffle of gravel, as someone walked towards me. No matter what, even though I was expecting to see Elijah, I felt a quick chill shoot down my spine. It's an unnerving feeling being alone in a pitch black area. I've seen horrible things happen to people and heard many other stories; I refuse to be another statistic.

But there he was, that familiar figure emerging from the shadows. I actually had to push back the giggle about to escape my mouth as I watched Elijah walking towards me in all of his glory. He was always so predictable, with his Bose headphones attached to his ears – music was definitely a big deal to him: hip-hop to be exact. His clothes were always nicely pressed and he never left home without a gold chain around his neck. Fake, of course.

I will never forget how remarkably sweet and caring he was when he gave me my new blanket. He seemed a little embarrassed because he wouldn't look me in the face as he threw this bag on the ground in front of me and unzipped it, revealing a blanket. My blanket.

That was the sweetest thing anyone has ever done for me. It might sound lame, but it's true. The blanket is huge and made out of fleece, so it does the job, you know? Immediately I got rid of my ratty old blanket. I'd used that one for a year, so it was a giant mess. There were big holes which let in all the cold air, making the comfort of warmth hard to come by.

It was that night that I really began to think that I might have liked Elijah. I couldn't get over the feeling of it being weird though. We were really good friends and I didn't want to ruin that. I couldn't help but find him attractive, even through his forced 'tough guy' demeanour. It was humorous actually, because deep inside he really was a sensitive and caring guy – not tough at all. The sad thing is, I never did get to tell him...

Where was I? Oh yeah, how everything changed.

Elijah was a talker, rarely giving me any time to speak about anything. I didn't mind it though; it often made me feel like I had a normal life, even if only for a moment. Sometimes he would go on and on about his life at home, and how he couldn't stand his father. I didn't understand that either, because in truth, his dad cared about him and was only being protective. That isn't a bad thing. He talked about girls sometimes too, which never failed to make me laugh. He acted as if he was the next Don Juan.

That night Elijah was talking about something completely different, though. It's been over a year since I have been in school and I actually miss it, so when he started talking about wanting to quit I couldn't understand. He only had a year left until he would have graduated, but he thought that he could make a good living out on the streets, that an education didn't really matter.

Thirty minutes went by fast, and by the end of our conversation I was scared. Scared for him and what he wanted to do with his life. But what could I have done? I didn't have the right to preach to him about what was right or wrong because, let's face it, I work on the streets seven nights a week. I should have preached to him, though – and maybe then he would have made it.

Anyway, after Elijah rambled on about his goals in life, he made it known that he wanted to work for Big Jon. I told him upfront that I thought it was a horrible idea and that he could get hurt. He thought that he could handle it and be successful. In my eyes, selling drugs is by no means being successful, but out here, when someone has their mind set on something, they do it. I thought that if I didn't help Elijah, he would try to take it into his own hands – and that scared me.

I'm not close to Big Jon in any way, but we are at least acquaintances and Elijah knew that. I have spoken to him in passing during the midnight hours plenty of times, and he has always been polite to me in his own way. Of course he holds no respect for anyone like me; that's the way it works, I know that.

That night I made the worst mistake by telling Elijah that I would talk to Jon. I seriously didn't think Jon would go for it, though, and so felt quite safe making that promise. Also, I guess I was afraid that I would lose Elijah as a friend if I didn't. That was a stupid way to think. He probably would've understood. Maybe he would still be here today, sitting next to me, joking around the way we always did. I can't help but blame myself.

I really need to snap out of it! With all of the thinking about that particular night, I've ruined my buzz, and now it's already time for me to go to work.

Normally my high doesn't make me obsess about any certain thing, but lately I can't help it. I just miss him so much. The only friend I ever had.

CHAPTER 3

Walking to work isn't exciting either. There is nothing spectacular to see, it's miserable. The street lights are dim and the cobblestone roads are filled with trash in this part of town. It's as if this area is forgotten, far from the world of executives, desperate housewives and children at play. It appears to be a ghost town, except for the gang of men and young boys joking and carrying on by City Liquors, and clown-faced women who are walking around in six-inch heels, looking for a catch.

Getting through the night feels like forever sometimes, evoking misery and the anxiety that I've managed to hide all day long. At night, I must become someone that I'm not. But I guess that after a year of being out here on the streets, I really am that other person.

Most nights it takes at least an hour of standing at my post on the corner of Benz Street until work starts coming my way. I call it work for a few reasons. One being because it sounds more appealing – to me. What I do disgusts me, so it is a lot of work on my part to make it through the night.

The other women that walk this street don't seem to mind their job at all. They happily talk to one another and speak to every man that drives their way. It takes me a while to ground myself, control my mind and become appealing to those who pass by.

I don't have a certain technique, but I do have something the other women on this block don't – I'm young and reasonably attractive. I lie about my age frequently. I have even managed to get away with being twenty-one years old, when I am really only sixteen. I would never get any clients if I was honest about my age. Besides, this job isn't about honesty, it's about money and that's it. There is no satisfaction.

Once I manage to get over the nauseating feeling in my stomach, I am able to make myself available. I will walk towards the street and down the sidewalk at a slow pace in a way that I would normally not walk. I have to actually concentrate on swaying my hips for appeal. I gaze into almost every car that slows down when passing, batting my eyes and smiling in a way that is sure to catch someone's eye.

As horrifying as it may sound, I do have a couple of regular clients. It doesn't make the job any better, it still disgusts me, but at least I know what they are about and how they treat girls like me. They also don't make me do anything out of the ordinary, like some men do. People are sick and want what they want, sometimes the unspeakable. I guess that's why they come to the block, instead of asking their girlfriends or wives – which many of our clients do have. If their wives knew what they were doing, they'd be devastated.

I am getting off track. The point is, it's a horrible job and I am ashamed to announce what I do. But, just in case I haven't been very clear, I'm a prostitute. I never in my wildest dreams would have imagined I'd end up out here on the streets like this. When I ran away from home a year ago, I had a plan – and this was not it. But life is hard. Survival is the key and I was starving, freezing and withering away to nothing. I did what was needed to survive – and still do.

It has been a slow night tonight, with no work for at least two hours. There are normally close to ten girls out on the block, but tonight there are maybe six of us out here. I think Michelle, the oldest, is the only one who has been picked up. In many ways I am relieved, yet at the same time I'm really in need of some money. I haven't managed to eat anything all day and I need a shower. If I gather enough money tonight, I can get a cheap room during the day tomorrow and clean up a little. I need it, bad.

Through the thick fog that has settled in, I manage to see a set of headlights coming my way. When the car slows down and pulls up to the curb next to me, I can tell by the outer appearance that the driver is probably hideous. I have learned over the past year that a car actually says a lot about a person. The chocolate brown, beat up and rusted El Camino looks about fifty years old, and cars like that are never a good sign.

I walk over to the car with my lips curled and a scandalous smile upon my face. I place my hands above the passenger side window and bend down, revealing my cleavage and face to the driver. At first, I can not see his face because he leans over to wind down the window. Once he does, the scent of stale cigar smoke and rotten fast food reaches my nostrils quickly. I try hard to stand my ground, seeming interested in the overweight, unshaven and obviously unclean man who is looking up at me. His smile only makes his appearance worse.

His teeth are chipped and rotten, which I am sure is not helping the smell that seems to surround me.

I bend down even closer to the window and give him a quick wink. With that, he jolts with excitement.

"You lookin' for some fun tonight?" I ask, while quickly stroking his arm.

It is always best to tease the men a little bit, give them a small taste of what's to come. This almost guarantees that they will want your services. Anyway, once I touch his sweaty arm he surely is ready to get me into his Camino.

"Get on in here," is all he says to me, as I open his rickety door and sit down on the coffee-stained seat.

He decides to drive a couple of miles down the road to the cheapest motel on this side of town. Even though it's only a short distance to the motel, it feels like an eternity. Every time I look over at him, his beady eyes are focused on me. Of course, I try to keep his attention by occasionally touching his leg or giving him a flirtatious wink, but honestly, his gaze makes me feel a bit sick.

The Sunny Days Motel isn't charming in any way. It looks more like a roach hotel. I don't even know how it stays open, because there are always vacancies – there are never more than three cars in the lot. The rooms always smell like mildew and the beds are very old and worn out. None of this matters to me though; it's not like I'm going on a summer vacation. I will go in, do what needs to be done and hopefully leave within the hour. I only give my customers an hour, unless they are paying me very well.

After he parks his car, I get out and wait for him to return with the key. Ten minutes seem to pass until I see him walking towards me. In those ten minutes I have been able to smoke a couple of cigarettes and touch up my makeup. I only started smoking a few weeks ago. I realised that it helps calm my nerves, because even though I appear serene and collected on the outside, I am truly full of anxiety.

As he gets closer to me, I am able to see the grin on his face. He is like a kid in a candy shop, anticipating the moment he will get his goodies. I walk towards him a bit, smiling and once again giving him a flirtatious wink.

"All set, sexy?" I ask, getting even closer to his sweaty body and putting my fingers through his hair.

Not a word escapes his mouth, but his body language says it all. He flashes the room key and then walks a few steps down to room number eight. I stand back only a little and rub his back as he wiggles the key to open the door.

Once the room is revealed, my stomach turns. I walk in behind him, take off my heels and close the door. He quickly sits on the bed and stares directly at me with the most sickening look upon his face. I hope the next hour passes quickly – yuck.

Chapter Three

It took me an hour and a half to get back to Benz Street. He ended up dropping me off two blocks away, and why wouldn't he, considering he'd got what he wanted, right? Like I said before, I don't expect any of my customers to respect me. Anyway, once I make it back to my post there is only one girl left on the block. Two in the morning is the witching hour out here. You never know if work will pick up or stay at a standstill. I don't mind waiting a while to be picked up again though – I need time to rejuvenate.

The man who picked me up earlier was pretty gross, but at least he wasn't asking for anything out of the ordinary. I managed to weasel thirty bucks out of him, so even if I don't come across more work tonight, at least I will have enough cash to check into a roach motel for a quick shower tomorrow. Or maybe grab a bite to eat.

Every night I manage to stick to one major rule in the hope of keeping myself reasonably safe. Some girls out here don't have any self-appointed guidelines, which I think is crazy. They all tell me that keeping any restrictions on what I am willing to do will make me lose money in the end. I don't care though, I'd rather be safe – protection is always needed. One day I am getting out of here, and I don't want to go into the real world with some sort of STD or a kid in tow.

Most nights, Benz Street is full of ruckus. Often the noise comes from a group of guys standing across the street drinking liquor and fooling around or fighting. Occasionally I get pestered by an addict of some sort, or the homeless, asking me for money. But tonight it is very quiet.

I will be out here for another hour or two, hopefully getting a little more work. I try to leave the area before dawn, avoiding any police officers that might pass through.

I'm not sure what I am going to do yet. It's a hard decision. Do I shower and rest, and starve for the day? Or get a little bit of food? Sometimes it is hard to decide between the two. Showering is needed, and meth and food don't really go together.

One thing crosses my mind though; if I do go see Jonah again tomorrow I can probably score some food, which would save me for the day, making it possible to get a room and shower. I don't know, though. I'm not so sure it's worth it, having to tell him all the sappy stories of my life. Also, I don't see how revealing my past to him makes a difference in him helping me. I didn't say I wanted his help anyway.

CHAPTER 4

I stopped at a little sandwich shop on my way back at about four in the morning. The shop isn't twenty-four hours, but opens at the crack of dawn. It's very small and doesn't get a lot of custom, which I like. I try to stay away from places that are filled with people, because they look at me as if I have the plague or something. My breakfast of choice is a bagel with sausage, egg and cheese. It fills my stomach and is dirt cheap, coming to only five dollars with a drink.

Once I get back to the bridge I grab my bag, which is hidden behind a slab of broken-down cement. There is nothing spectacular in there that anyone would want to take, but I hide it anyway. It holds all the necessities, my toothbrush, toothpaste and some shampoo that I stole from a luxury hotel a few weeks back. Oh, and Elijah's blanket.

It has become a habit for me to take in a line or two before I take a nap each morning. Honestly, it's the only thing that relaxes me enough to even try to sleep. It only takes five minutes or less for me to enter a euphoric state of being. Without that I would obsess about my night's work and the disgusting men I came across. Before I found meth, it was hard for me to even think about sleeping.

By the time I cover myself with the blanket and get comfortable, my eyes begin to feel heavy. I never sleep more than a few hours because I've learnt to quickly rest, and then move on for the day.

I've never been caught sleeping out here, and I don't want to risk it either. I really shouldn't call it sleep. It's more like resting my eyes. It's never happened, but you never know when some weirdo or crackhead may wander over my way, and I'd surely want to be awake for that! A little sleep is better than no sleep though, right?

After a while, an odd sensation comes upon me. I know that I am lying here with my eyes closed, sleeping. But I feel like I'm awake. I feel everything that is happening as I fall into a vivid and surreal dream-like state.

No matter how hard I try, I can't stop it.

I know that I am in a small room, but I don't recognise it. It's dark – too dark – and I feel utterly alone, even though a presence is with me. This presence isn't pleasant, though. Nothing in this room is. There isn't any kind of familiarity, just dark shadows that seem to hover above.

At first I realise that the room is empty, except for the small bed that I am lying on. I try to scream, but I can't. Not a sound escapes my mouth, even though it is open. Tears flow as I jerk my body to escape the shadows that come near me. They are not happy, whatever they are.

A flash of a wooded area then comes into view. It looks familiar, but I can't quite make out where I am, as I lay in the brush. The trees are swaying with force, screaming out to me, telling me to run while I can. But I can't. The trees come alive as tiny branches wrap around my ankles and wrists, forcing me to stay on the ground.

The shadows have followed me into this dark wooded area now. Their laughter is almost demented as they come into view. They are pushing me down too, laying on me, forcing me to be immersed in their dark silhouettes.

I smell it. Their stench resembles the smell of old, rotten beer – it seems to consume my entire being. They don't stop either. They only push me lower into the ground, forcing themselves upon me. I squirm. I shake, trying to escape. Maybe I should scream?

I manage to make a sound that echoes through the trees. The branches loosen their grip and I somehow manage to pull myself away from the shadows. Again I scream, even louder than before.

I now hover above them. Looking down I see the one shadow begin to morph itself into human form. It's Johnny. His dark, angry eyes seem to pierce my skin and his demented laugh only gets louder as he reaches for me. Not again! I scream.

I wake up under my blanket, screaming for my life. Sweat pours off me and tears fall quickly from my makeup-smeared eyes. I quickly touch my face to make sure that I am really here, underneath the bridge, far from my past, far away from Johnny.

What the hell was that? I can't remember the last time I've had a nightmare that extreme, especially about Johnny. Not for years, I'd say. Why would I even dream up such a thing? Why now?

That damn Jonah, he brought this to the surface! What good is that? I was managing well without the memory, and now it's here with me again. See, that's why I don't know if a visit to Jonah this afternoon is such a good idea. I mean, maybe he can help me – but do I really need it? And why is he stirring up old memories, things I'd rather just forget about? If you ask me, it's not a good thing at all. It will probably only make me feel worse.

The only reason that I would go see him today is for the food. If I manage to take in a good hearty dinner, I will be set until tomorrow afternoon. Whatever saves money works for me. I hear the City Community Center has great meals sometimes, like fried chicken and beef stew. And I miss fried chicken. I'm not quite sure yet, but I may go down there later this afternoon after all.

Until then, I'm not sure what I will do. I might go to the park and take a walk. It's never too crowded there, so I don't draw attention to myself. Drawing attention to me is one thing I really try not to do. I can't handle all the empty stares and implied criticism. I may look funny in my ratty clothing, but I'm still a human being with feelings.

The park is huge. It holds a giant pond where many ducks and geese rest. It might sound lame, but I like to sit on the benches and watch them as they go about their day. It relaxes me a little, I guess. They are so innocent and free, and don't need to worry about anything. And if they get tired of where they are, they simply fly away. I wish I could do that. Fly away to a place where I can be normal again, or anywhere I want for that matter.

Some days I try to go to the library. Well, I think about going, but never do. Again, strangers stare too much and it makes me uncomfortable. It is probably weird for them, though, seeing me. I guess it's abnormal to see a prostitute picking up a book or two, but there is no law saying that because I work on the streets I can't read. Although I'm sure many can't.

I miss reading. I haven't picked up a book in over a year. Books used to be my escape. Now I have no escape whatsoever, just reality. The reality of my life isn't so great, but there's nothing I can do about that right now. It is what it is.

Hours have passed, and I'm on my way to the Community Center. I'm not looking forward to it. I hate the walls of Jonah's office. They feel like they close in on me, and I'm not looking forward to his stupid questions, either. But right now that doesn't matter. I need something to eat and I'd rather not pay for it if I don't have to.

The walk to the Center is a little unpleasant, because I have to pass through the poor side of the city, where everyone avoids eye contact. People have been killed out here, just because they might have looked at someone the wrong way. I've never had a problem, though – I just make sure that I keep my eyes to the ground.

It's sad actually. I hear this area used to be the centre of entertainment. Music shops, coffee houses and diners attracted many, before the crime rate increased and a group of gangs moved in. Most of the gangs out this way are affiliated with Big Jon's business – another reason why I try to walk unnoticed.

He has a secluded warehouse a few blocks down from the centre. A warehouse that holds pounds upon pounds of cocaine and meth, not to mention a load of weapons. As far as I know he has never been spotted by the authorities, so I guess his tactics work – as far as him staying hidden is concerned.

I managed to see the inside of his warehouse once. Of course Elijah was in there loads of times, once he started working for Jon. How I wish I could turn back the hands of time, but it's too late for that now.

It was about two months ago when Elijah and I walked into that warehouse. Two long months ago.

On the night before the meeting I ran into Jon on the corner of Benz Street where I was working. Secretly I prayed that I wouldn't ever see him again. I didn't want to go out of my way to hook Elijah up with him. But no such luck.

I remember it well, because work was scarce that night. It was too quiet. Most of the girls on my block walked to another area where they were sure they could find work. But I decided to stay. It's always better for me to work alone anyway. Steering clear of a group of girls makes it much easier for me to get picked up anyway, and yet stay unnoticed.

That night, a couple of hours passed until I heard the sound of life. A sound system was blaring and only got louder as a black Cadillac Escalade crept towards the intersection where I was standing. It was so loud, in fact, that I could feel the vibration of the bass against my skin.

I knew who owned the truck right away, with its chrome twenty inch rims and dark, tinted windows – Big Jon. He is the only person out on this block to own a decent car. Everyone else either uses public transportation or travels on foot. This is another reason why he stands out in the neighbourhood.

Anyway, he parked his Cadillac a few feet away from me, with the stereo system still blaring. Two young kids dressed in black, probably no more than seventeen years old, walked across the street to greet him. Jon stepped out of the car and talked to the boys briefly, before they handed over two brown paper bags. I figured the kids probably worked for him and were handing over their daily earnings.

Jon is in no way suffering for money. He takes the majority of the earnings, only leaving a small percentage for his workers. But when you are a kid, that small percentage seems like a lot of dough. That is exactly what Elijah thought, not thinking about the consequences. Money seems to rule the world.

After the kids left, I couldn't help myself. I gathered enough courage to talk to him. He didn't notice me at first because he was busy stashing something in his truck. I decided to walk towards him, in the hope that he would realise I was there. It only took a moment.

"Damn, girl! I didn't see you standin' there," he said, as if shocked to see me. "You quiet as a mouse," he said, setting his baseball cap straight. "Gettin' work?"

"Nothin' to brag about," I remember saying. "Tonight is slower than ever. How's your business?"

"You know everything is always gravy, baby!" he replied with a chuckle.

We talked briefly about nothing remotely serious. I remember him joking around about my work in a way that irritated me, but I didn't dare show that it was getting to me.

While we were talking, Elijah kept coming to mind. I really didn't want to help him get into trouble with Jon, but that was his decision, right? I should've stood my ground, but I didn't. I wanted to give Elijah what he wanted, just because I wanted to please him.

Before Jon got back into his Escalade, I decided to ask him if he was looking for help. At first he thought that I was inquiring for myself, which only made him laugh. He told me that he didn't work with tricks. I hate that word.

I had to force myself to laugh along with him for a minute, before telling him that I was asking for a friend of mine. He seemed to be a little leery about the idea, but agreed to meet with Elijah the following night to talk. He knew I was someone who kept my head down, kept out of trouble. I guess he thought Elijah would be the same. Then, he looked dead serious.

"You better not be playin' with me," he said.

The tone of his voice made my insides turn. I was scared for Elijah, and even then that should've given me a fair warning about what could happen – and what eventually did happen.

I really have to stop thinking about it, but I can't. It's my fault Elijah is gone.

CHAPTER 5

Jonah decides to let me eat alone in his office, before he will once again start badgering me about my past. I haven't figured out if talking about it is a good thing or a bad thing. So many memories are ones I'd rather keep hidden, because I don't want to feel that pain all over again.

The walls aren't welcoming, seeming even colder than before. My anxiety is already building, causing my skin to crawl. Part of me wants to run out of here. Who's to say he will help me? Besides, no one in my entire lifetime has cared about what happens to me; how is this going to be different? Initially someone may seem to be devoted to helping kids, or helping anyone in general for that matter. But when it gets too tough, they walk away and never look back – in my experience anyway.

By the time Jonah walks in to his office I am on my last piece of chicken. I ate more food today than I have in a long time, which has caused me to feel a bit nauseous. Actually, I'm not sure whether it's the large amount of food that's made me feel sick, or the thought of having to relive the memories.

He sits behind his desk paging through a spiral bound notebook, finally stopping once he reaches a blank page.

"I'm so glad you decided to come see me again Savannah," he smiles. "I was hoping you would."

I adjust myself in the chair, slumping down even more.

"Thanks for the chicken."

"The chicken is one of my favorite choices that they have here. Of course, if you eat it every day it gets boring fast," he laughs.

I didn't laugh, nor smile. I don't care if he likes the chicken. What's the point in small talk? Just get to it, so I can get out of here. Or at least tell me what you think you can do for me. What's the use in dragging it out?

"So I'd like to hear a little more about you, Savannah. Your past, and how you ended up out here," he finally says. "I have a couple hours, so maybe we can finish this up today, so tomorrow I can try to find you a place somewhere. If you'd like."

"I don't know what you want me to say," I respond.

"The truth about you."

"I don't know, man – I mean it's nothin' great, and I don't know what you are gonna do for me," I say.

"Well even if you decide you don't want my help, it's good to talk. But I want to help you."

Is he a joke? I guess I can't say much, because I am sitting in this office. I didn't have to come. Maybe a part of me believes that he can help me, but another part of me tells me to run away fast. That's all I ever do, though. Maybe it's time for me to change a little. I don't know.

I'm not sure where I left off the last time I was here. I get mixed up often, and my mind has been playing tricks on me lately. I think I was talking about nasty Johnny, and leaving my mama's house.

Once I left Mama I was immediately placed at Cedar Farm's Home for Girls. Obviously it was new to me and I was scared to death. I did miss my mama, but the relief at not having to face more abuse from Johnny somehow made up for that. I

didn't know what to expect either or how I
would get along with everyone, because I'd
never been liked by anyone.

Cedar Farm is about five hours from
the city, in the middle of nowhere. The
building looked more like a log home, and
didn't seem big enough for the fifteen girls
it housed. It was surrounded by trees, on
a large amount of land. I don't know how
much, but the yard never seemed to end,
no matter how deep into the woods you
travelled. The immediate backyard was
a playground, with swings and a hamster
wheel – which was my favorite. It also had
a separate building which was used as a
school for us girls.

The range of ages varied, from seven
years old to twelve. Their hope at the
farm was to have everyone adopted, so we
wouldn't have to be placed at another home,
a foster home, when we reached thirteen.
The idea wasn't bad, but in my entire time
there I only saw one girl get taken in by a
family.

The workers there weren't the greatest either. It seemed to be a task for them to work with us, as if they just wanted to go home to be with their families. That's how I felt anyways.

Once I got there I was looked at as the outcast immediately. No one wanted to be my friend. They all stayed in their groups and laughed at me, joking about how no one wanted me. That comment stuck with me every day, even though I didn't understand how they could say such a thing, because they were at the same place I was. But at nine years old those comments can really dig deep and stay there for good.

We had daily chores, which weren't so bad I guess. We were assigned to different jobs every week, like cleaning the main bathroom or our living quarters. Somehow, I ended up doing most of it, being bullied by Endya who beat me up quite a few times.

Endya was a very big ten year old who had a horrible attitude. She ran the place, managing to keep everyone else as her friend. She would order the other girls around and told them to stay away from me. Why? Because I was ugly. I don't remember how that came about, but it was like that until she left.

In comparison with all the other kids I wasn't so different, so I don't know why I was the one being called ugly – they didn't look all that pleasant either. Granted, at first I did have mismatched clothing and was the smallest of the group, with long scrawny legs that peeked out through the bottom of my pants. Eventually the staff bought me some new clothing, so I didn't look that bad anymore.

I would say my time there was mostly horrible, but only because of Endya. Right when I woke up she would start with me, laughing and pointing, and forcing me to do her work – if I didn't, she would beat me up.

Sometimes at lunch she would knock my plate out of my hands. I would stand there utterly embarrassed as the food went crashing to the floor. Often tears filled my eyes, but I would force them back – if only to avoid even more laughter from all the girls who were staring at me.

My memories tend to run together, but from the time I spent at the Farm, one major event stands out. Of course, it had to do with Endya.

It was around lunch time when it happened. It's hard to remember what day it was, but I know it was on a weekend, because I was outside cleaning up the leaves on the playground. I was minding my own business when Endya came around, knocking over the leaves that I had neatly pushed into a pile. I stood there with the rake in my hand, avoiding eye contact. I learned fast that if you don't make eye contact, they will more than likely go away or leave you alone.

Anyway, after she knocked over the leaves I'd just raked, she stood there staring at me with an almost evil grin on her face.

"Hey, chicken legs."

I didn't respond. I stood there gazing at nothing really, my eyes to the ground.

"Did you hear me talking to you? You better listen to me before I knock your teeth out!"

I finally got the nerve to look at her, but only briefly. "What's up, Endya?" I said, trying not to sound irritated.

"Oh nothin', just seeing what you were doing."

I knew something was up because she would never, ever talk to me if she wasn't planning something.

"What does it look like I'm doing?" I said, before I could shove the words back into my mouth. That was the wrong thing to say. She was in front of my face within a couple of seconds.

"You better not be getting smart with me, you bastard." She grabbed my shirt, pulling my face right against hers. "Because you know I will hurt you," she continued. A cocky grin stayed on her face. I knew it pleased her to get a rise out of me, so I tried to remain calm.

"I'm sorry Endya. I'm just tired of these leaves, not sure why I have to be the one to rake them every weekend," I said, hoping to calm the air. "What's up?"

"Oh nothin' really, I just wanted to show you something really cool I found in the woods," she said. "I didn't know that anyone else lived around here, but I found a house down the way yesterday."

"Yeah?"

"Yep. I saw a coupla kids playing in the backyard with some frogs, too – just wanted to show ya."

"Frogs?"

"I think they are their pets, they're awesome-looking!"

"How'd you see them? We can't go in their house or anything."

"Nah. They are outside. Wanna look?"

"I dunno, it's almost lunch. We'll get in trouble."

"No we won't, they won't even notice. And besides, you don't have a choice. I will beat the shit outta you."

I stood there for a moment, not knowing what to do. What was she gonna do with those frogs? And why even go see them at all? I was sure she could find her own frogs if we took a trip to the stream nearby. But no matter how badly I didn't want to go – I didn't have a choice.

We walked for a while. It felt like forever to me, because I had a bad feeling about the whole thing. She pulled me the entire way.

She held my arm with one hand, and in the other there was a giant screwdriver. That was why I knew something was weird. I didn't want to get into trouble, but obviously she didn't care.

The tiny cottage was built out of bricks, and it looked a hundred years old. If it wasn't for a swing set in the backyard and smoke escaping the mouth of the chimney, I would've sworn it was abandoned. The grass was a tiny bit overgrown too, giving the entire property an eerie feeling.

Endya ducked down quickly once we approached the chain-linked fence. It's not like anyone couldn't see us, with the gaping holes in it – maybe she thought she was invisible. Anyway, I stood next to a tree and watched her from afar, until she ran up to me and grabbed my arm, pulling me to the fence.

"What are you doing? You gotta help me," she said.

"What are ya trying to do?" I asked, slightly scared of what her response might be.

"I told you, we're gonna get the damn frogs!"

"Get them?"

"Yes, you idiot!"

"I don't think—"

"You don't think what?" she interrupted. "You are gonna climb over and open the door with this screwdriver."

"Me? Why me? Why don't you do it?"

She grabbed my shirt again and threw me up against the fence, hard. "You are getting them," she said, "and don't worry, they aren't home, I already checked."

My stomach hurt badly and my nerves were shot. I didn't want to go to jail for stealing some stupid frogs; I'd watched enough television to know what jail looked like – and it wasn't for me. I was scared, but what was I to do? Endya held her fists up to me as a warning, and I didn't doubt that she would hit me.

To cut a long story short, I stole two frogs from their shed in the backyard. With some effort and ten minutes or so of panic I managed to take the screws from the wooden door of the shed.

I probably should have checked the door first before taking it off, though. There was no need for the entire door to fall to the ground, because it was already unlocked. I could have saved a lot of time by just opening the door and grabbing the frogs, but I had to do what Endya told me.

The entire time she stood on the other side of the fence threatening me with her fists and intimidating gaze. I don't know why I was such a coward when it came to her. Maybe I wanted her to like me, and

I thought that if I did what she said, she would stop bullying me so much. Whatever the reason was, she scared me.

We walked back to Cedar Farm with a frog in each of our hands, but we didn't get too far before we were caught. Whoever lived at the cottage had followed us halfway back home. We heard someone angrily yelling at us to get our attention, but we ignored it and kept on walking.

I'm sure they knew where we were going, seeing as we were young girls and no one else lived in the area. With that said, we were in trouble right away when we walked into the lunchroom.

When we walked through the doors my stomach dropped. One of the lead counsellors and an older-looking woman I'd never seen before were standing together talking. Michelle, our counsellor, looked upset and stopped in mid-sentence once she saw Endya and me.

I was blamed for the entire affair. Endya cried to Michelle, saying that I forced her, when really it was the other way around. She was such a liar. I'm not sure how she got away with everything she did, but she surely did – always.

The older woman didn't press charges for us stealing her grandchildren's frogs, but told Michelle that if anything like that ever happened again, she would go to the authorities. I didn't think frogs were a reason to go to jail, but at that age I wasn't sure how everything worked. Instead of jail time, I had a load of chores to do that entire month, without any play time.

I stayed at the Farm for three more years after that day. Nothing changed, even when Endya left to go to a foster home. I was still bullied and laughed at, and had no friends. Almost every night I cried myself to sleep. I didn't understand why I was so hated or disliked.

After all, I didn't do anything to make people hate me. I would have done anything to have someone love me – but that wasn't in my cards, I guess.

CHAPTER 6

Jonah sits at his desk eagerly awaiting more of my story. I feel like I've told him enough. I don't see how any more of this crap is going to make him decide on whether or not to help me. Didn't he already say he would? Then why all of this torture?

Next thing I know he's going to get out that stupid board game on his desk. It's a dumb game that is supposed to make someone want to talk. I think we are way past that point, but maybe not. I keep seeing his eyes lock onto the cardboard box it's in. There is no way I am playing that. He's out of his mind.

Only forty-five minutes have passed since I started talking to him, rambling on about my messed up life. But really that's it.

"That can't be it, Savannah," he starts again. "Where did you go from Cedar Farm? How did you end up out here?"

This feeling of annoyance and aggravation is beginning to brew within. I feel like I should leave now, but something inside me must want to talk, because I stay.

Where did I go after leaving the Farm? It closely compares to this hell-hole I call the street. It's too bad that I had to live there for three years before realising how badly I needed to get away and be on my own. After all, I wasn't really being taken care of – so why not take care of myself? That's how I saw it anyway. Still, to this day I'm glad I left.

Miss Peters was a recently widowed, angry soul. For whatever reason, she never managed to birth her own children, which probably explained her bitter attitude towards me. Her hair was graying, but other than that she looked reasonably young. I'd guess that she was probably in her forties. Anyway, I was her first foster child.

I didn't know then, but the state paid for her to keep me. It wasn't a large amount of money, but enough for her to gobble it up, leaving nothing left for my care. I'm sure there are people out there who genuinely want to help those forgotten children, but there's also a fair few who are only in it for the money. Miss Peters was one of those people, even though she was already rich. So why was she worried about a measly grand?

When she and I first met, I thought it was going to be great, being the first time someone would actually care about me. In front of my social worker she was as nice as could be, very caring and lovable towards me – like nothing else mattered to her in the world.

She walked me up to my new bedroom, filled with toys of all sorts. There were Barbies, stuffed animals and a gigantic dollhouse. I tried to hold it in, but I cried tears of joy. I couldn't believe what I was seeing. Without thinking, I hugged Miss Peters tightly, very tightly – my social worker had to peel me away. But Miss Peters didn't seem to mind my hug then, with her smiling face and glistening eyes. To me, she was beautiful. My new mom.

For the first time in my life, I was happy. That happiness blinded me too, causing me to ignore all of the signs that easily revealed that things were about to change. Within two weeks Miss Peters was a different woman, and not for the better. It was an abrupt, odd transformation. Maybe initially she was trying to appear friendly, so that the state would allow her to be a foster parent – so that she could get a monthly paycheck. Who knows?

Overall I guess her behavior wasn't too cruel, she just became completely withdrawn – from me and everyone else in her life. Maybe she should've let me go somewhere else, but she didn't. She kept me there, feeding on her misery. As time went on, instead of getting better, she spiraled downhill.

While I lived there, it was hard for me to tell if she was naturally miserable or just temporarily depressed. But now I really believe she was born a selfish and mean human being. How she acted towards me only revealed that truth. I don't know how any man could have put up with her.

Jonah is still staring at me with that same stupid look on his face.

My skin begins to crawl. I feel like I'm getting off track, but I can't help it. My mind is racing, making it difficult to gather any thoughts, and my anxiety has kicked in. I'm ready to leave this cold office and never return.

My hands are shaking, sweat is seeping through my pores and I feel like I'm about to lose it. Why is he still staring at me like that? Can't he tell I'm having a panic attack? He probably wouldn't care if I dropped dead right now. One less kid on the street, huh? One less junkie to worry about. That's not me.

I can't hold it back anymore...

"Why all these damn questions?" I yell. "You have been sitting in the same position this entire time, looking at me with that pathetic look on your face!" I try to calm down, but I can't. I can't breathe, my heart is racing and I am angry – angrier than I've been in a long time.

"Calm down, Savannah," Jonah says to me quietly. "It's going to be okay, I can help you if you let me."

"You can help me? How the hell are you gonna help me? You don't even know me!"

"I'm trying to get to know you, so I will know the right way to help."

"Bullshit. You want to laugh at me, point at me, use me as an example for all those broads on the street," I yell even louder. "I'm not them! And it's not my damn fault that this is how I ended up, either!"

"No one is blaming you."

I breathe heavily as I pace the room. I see people staring through the glass windows, and I stare back, throwing them a finger that no one would appreciate.

"Calm down," he continues. "You don't have to tell me any more if you don't want to right now, okay?" He closes the blinds on the windows, hoping to distract my vision from those who were staring.

"I gotta go," I say, placing my hand on the doorknob. "You wanna know what happened with Miss Peters?" I ask angrily as I swing open his door, almost knocking it off the hinges.

"Only if you want to tell me. Please, sit back down."

"All I gotta say is that no one – and I mean *no one* – can handle someone telling you all the time that you are a stupid, unwanted and pathetic girl. So, I left."

"She called you that?"

"Every day, unless she was ignoring me," I respond. "But if anyone else came around, she loved me dearly."

"Want to tell me more?"

"Nope, that's it. I'm outta here. Everyone in my life has been nothing but fake, except one – so, how can I trust you?" I ask, stomping out of his office.

As I walk away, I faintly hear his voice yell out, "Tomorrow morning if you want, Savannah. You can trust me."

But the thing is, I don't know if I can...

CHAPTER 7

As I walk away from the City Community Center, I still feel it. I still feel the rage that's brewing inside. It needs to escape, but is unable to reach the surface as anger, instead becoming a river of tears.

The memories of my life surface all at once, causing my whole being to feel completely numb. I could shut down, I need to shut down. The bridge by Flannigan's is too far to walk. I won't make it – I need it now. I need a fix.

Everything I'm passing is blurred, like it doesn't exist, as my mind remains fixed on that day I left Miss Peters' house. We were fighting, badly. For two years I let her degrade me, call me names and ignore me as if I were invisible. That day something clicked – I realised it wasn't okay. The fury I'd held in for my entire life exploded.

At first I begged her to call my case worker and have me sent to another home. I asked her why she even bothered keeping me there for so long, and she couldn't even respond. It didn't make sense.

"Just call her," I yelled, "I don't understand why you are even keeping me here. You don't give a shit!"

"Watch that tone, young lady!"

"You watch it! I'm not taking it from you any more, I don't have to!"

"You ungrateful brat!" she yelled back.

Quick as a flash, I was in her face. "Ungrateful you say? You're a miserable old maid, who only cares about herself!"

"Oh is that right? And that's why I took you in, right? Because I only think about myself?"

"You're crazy! I'm getting' outta here. Can't take you anymore! Gonna call her myself, and tell her that you should never have any kids in your house."

"Go ahead and leave. And Savannah – who are they going to believe? Me? Or a poor, depressed child who no one wants? Your mama didn't want you, that's why they threw ya on me."

I couldn't resist – I pushed her into the wall, fast and hard, and I'm sure I hurt her. And right after that, I just left. I ended up not calling my case worker, because I figured that I wouldn't have any luck there anyway. They'd probably stick me in another hell-hole, and if they were going to do that, I might as well be living on my own.

Granted, this might not be the life I had hoped for, but it's okay for now. Better than places like that. And once I save enough money I'll get out of here for good.

―――――――――

Back to reality. I need it, my body needs it. It's a craving I can't deny, especially when I feel like this. I need some place to go, an empty alleyway, a parking lot – anywhere.

I'm shaking and everyone is staring at me. I should sneak some into my hands, just a tiny bit is all I need, enough to relax me. I need to relax and stop thinking so much. Stop it!

I walk into a dark alleyway. As the sun sets, most of it is hidden in the shadows. No one will notice me here; maybe I should stay until I go to work. It only has one entrance, which is good. And I can stay alert, just in case any lunatics pass by. Normally I wouldn't do this because I don't know this area all that well, but I don't care right now. I need to calm myself down.

The zip-locked bag that carries my powder is low, too low. I feel panicked, because it will only supply me for another day or two. Then what? I can't go to Jon for any, or any of his dealers. That's where I used to get a fix, but now I need to stay as hidden as possible. If they saw me, I'd be where Elijah is – dead.

I lean back against the brick wall and pour some powder into the palm of my hand. I place it under my nose and inhale. Again and again, until I feel its power taking over my body. I've never used so much at one time, but I need it. I need the calming sensation, the euphoric state of bliss to take me away from all of my past miseries and worries of the present.

My mind drifts slowly, and visions of my best friend begin to surface. I smile, forgetting for a moment that I will never hear his laugh again, remembering perfect moments, those days we would goof off for hours. I remember that certain day when his face revealed pure excitement, when he knew his life was going to change forever. On that day his smile lit up my heart, even though my heart felt, at the same time, pained.

When Elijah was still around, I would often go to his house while his dad was still at work and hang out for a while. He used to joke with me, saying I only loved him because of his bathroom. That wasn't true, but I surely did love using his shower.

His dad had just had the bathroom refinished, so it was a taste of luxury – for me, anyway. I'm sure Elijah took it for granted because he was used to having some of the finer things in life, but the spa tub and stand-up double-headed shower amazed me. I would've probably stayed in the shower forever if Elijah didn't force me to get out.

On that day, I went over to his house around four o'clock in the afternoon. I'd planned on going over a little earlier, but most of the time it was safe so long as I left before six. I never understood why, but Elijah tried to keep me away from his dad as much as he possibly could. I gathered that his dad was over-protective, and the idea of his son being friends with a prostitute wouldn't have gone over well.

I remember exactly what Elijah smelled like. We were never that close, but often enough I would have to use his body wash and lotion when I was there. I missed smelling like a girl, because I always ended up smelling like a mixture of Old Spice body and Coolwater, an odd combination. I miss that smell, his scent.

This particular day stands out more than others. We were sitting on his bed relaxing. I was reading some sort of magazine, probably Spin or something like that, and he was playing Grand Theft Auto. From the moment I went over there, I was having an internal struggle. I wasn't sure whether I should or shouldn't tell him about his meeting with Jon that night. Actually, I was surprised he didn't ask me about it first, considering how excited about it he was.

Once I'd made the decision to tell him about it, his excitement level shot up within seconds, and his smile lit up the room. Immediately he started dancing around in his way. I loved how he danced, even though he acted as if he was in a hip-hop video, with his headphones on, bouncing back and forth. It made me laugh. I never saw him so excited or happy about anything. I guess he knew what he wanted to do, even though it wasn't the right thing. I remember worrying that he was too naïve to be in the street world, but he felt he could handle it. And for a moment there, I allowed myself to be convinced that everything might be alright.

Before we left his house he changed his clothes at least ten times. I repeatedly told him that Big Jon wasn't going to care what he looked like, but he insisted I was wrong. He wanted to look the part, matching his entire outfit from head to toe.

I feel it creeping in slowly as the effect wears off, the feeling of internal chaos. My eyelids twitch, but I cannot open my eyes. My body squirms as I try my hardest to ignore the visions that flash through my mind. I can't wake myself up, I feel tranquilised, paralysed.

First, a flashback of our meeting with Jon surfaces – the beginning of what changed my and Elijah's lives forever. The beginning of addiction, of pain and death. I could have changed it. I could've talked Elijah out of it. Instead I went along. I killed him. He didn't know how rough the streets were. He thought it was business. Sure, it was business – but if you handle your business wrong, you could end up dead. Yes, and that's what happened. I killed him.

I'm unaware of the tears that are falling from my eyes. My memory takes me back to that night when we entered the dark and secluded warehouse...

We walked in silence on our way to meet Big Jon. I suppose we both had thoughts racing through our minds; I know I did – worry over not knowing how the night was going to work out. Elijah didn't seem nervous at all. If anything, he was still buzzing.

Elijah walked the entire way with a forced strut, music blaring through his headphones. I glanced over at him a few times, but he never noticed me. He was hypnotised by the lyrics of the songs, as he often was, and by what was about to happen. I could hear him practising lines, what he was going to say to Jon when he met him. It was like he thought he could conquer the world.

As Elijah and I reached the door in the rear, I was startled when a tall, overweight, rough-looking kid dressed in black swung open the door. The warehouse was larger than I'd expected it to be. It was huge, actually. Two of Jon's luxury cars were parked near the front of the building, next to the garage door.

The place was jumping with people, adolescents mostly. A handful of kids were sitting at long rectangular tables, wrapping up goods. There weren't any light drugs going on in that place, like marijuana – it was all cocaine-based, or meth.

A few moments passed before I heard Jon's deep, intimidating voice.

"Hey trick, let's see whatcha got here," he yelled across the room.

I looked around for Jon, not noticing him right away. He was standing along one of the walls with another big guy who could've passed for his brother.

All of a sudden, I felt like everyone in the room was watching us. It was a weird feeling, walking towards Jon, having the gaze from the others practically burning my skin. I guess it was only me that felt that way, though, because Elijah walked across that room with his head to the sky, like he was the next best thing.

"Hey Big Jon, I'm Jah," Elijah said, reaching his hand out to offer Jon a friendly shake.

Jon didn't speak for a minute, just looked Elijah up and down, from head to toe.

"First of all, you can call me Mr Big," he announced. "Second, don't even try to shake my hand, boy! I don't know you like that!"

"My bad, Mr Big," Elijah replied, putting his hands to his side.

The meeting lasted about an hour. Jon spoke with Elijah alone for a while and decided to give him a chance. Elijah could start the very next day. He was shown the ropes of the place, but guidelines were kept to a minimum. Jon basically told Elijah that he better never do him wrong. That is what he told all the boys who worked for him and with the reputation he had, no one in their right mind would even think of screwing him over.

I think at first he viewed Elijah as lame, not thinking that he had it in him, but then again if he did, it would only mean more money for Jon, and money is Jon's middle name.

My body squirms once more, as I'm trying to wake myself from my dream. I see Jon's face, his eyes meet mine. He is so close that I can hear his breathing. He is angry. I try to walk away, but can't.

This isn't real, but his words feel like a knife penetrating my skin. "I told you, trick – no mistakes! And you didn't listen to me. Those were the consequences."

My head jerks, sweat is dripping off my body. I try to ignore his comments.

"Your boy got what he deserved. You better watch your back," he laughed.

My head jerks again, this time spiraling me away from my dream, away from Jon. As I wake up I am confused, but quickly realise that Jon is nowhere to be found. Why did I dream that? I'm scared that he is going to find me and his stolen bag of drugs that I have in my hands.

A Forgotten Tomorrow

I wasn't going to do it, but I need another fix. I need to calm down before going into work, and I only have an hour.

I can't stay away from this calm feeling, even though it's brief. My dreams seem to be much more vivid than usual, and I don't understand why. Oh well, right now I can't worry about that.

I take in more, hoping it will take me away...

CHAPTER 8

I can't help but love the feeling meth brings to me. I was unsure of even trying it the first time and I don't like to admit it, but I've become increasingly dependent on the substance to carry me through each day.

I didn't see Elijah for a while, for at least three weeks after he began working with Jon. I felt lonely, and it was almost excruciating. In a way I'd probably got used to relying on Elijah and his company, so when the days passed by without me seeing him, I didn't know what to do.

A Forgotten Tomorrow

The day I first experimented with meth was around the first time I saw Elijah since our initial talk with Jon. I had managed to speak with him over the phone occasionally, but that didn't compare to how close we used to be. Anyway, it wasn't too often that I had spare change to pay for a pay phone.

It was freezing outside, which didn't help the unsettling feeling I had either. For those three weeks I went directly to the bridge by Flannigan's after work, and stayed there for most of the day. It was too cold to move, so I stayed under my blanket. Even so, the cold managed to sneak through the fabric, making my body feel tense and rigid.

I stole an old rusted barrel from the pub, which I used to keep me warm. I gathered trash from their dumpster – as gross as that sounds – and used it to light a fire. I would light my cigarette, and when I finished, I'd flick it into the tiny barrel that sat only a few feet from me. At first I was paranoid that a spark would fly out and catch me alight as I rested. But I got used to it.

I was excited to be seeing Elijah again and to hear his stories about how things were going with Jon, even though I still didn't agree with him working that way. I was bored too, and figured his company would take me out of the depressed state of mind I was in.

At that point work was very scarce, which left me very short when it came to money. I tried to stretch it out as much as I could, only eating once a day and maybe showering twice a week. That sounds gross, I know – but I needed to eat more than I needed to shower. I just got used to smelling like stale smoke and the old, overpowering smell of body spray.

As I tossed my finished cigarette into the trash-filled barrel, there was a whooshing sound as the garbage caught on fire. In the midst of the crackling flame, I heard footsteps crunching across the gravel.

His strut and confident grin was something I had missed, and until that day I hadn't realised how much. His Bose headphones were still attached to his ears, and his hands were in the air, motioning to the beat of the music. I remember laughing silently, thinking that some things will never change. His appearance had certainly changed though. He looked better than ever.

"My girl!" he shouted, once he noticed me sitting there watching him.

It was then that I felt myself looking at him in a way I shouldn't have, and I was positive my smile would reveal what I was feeling.

"Damn, Jah! Where have ya been?" I joked. "Really, I thought you disappeared off the face of the earth."

With his arms wrapped around me, I felt it. I felt everything. His absence somehow made my feelings for him grow into something more than just friends. I didn't want to let go of him, ever. But I had to.

"You know how it is, all work and no play," he said, while ending our embrace. He backed away from me a little, and in his suave way, brushed his hands against his shirt. "Notice anything different?"

For a moment all I could do was look at him. He looked good, really good. His new, white hooded sweatshirt made his long, gold necklace and diamond stud stand out.

"New clothes I take it?"

"Yep. And this," he said, pointing to his ear.

"I noticed. Is that real?"

"You are asking me if it's real?" he laughed, "Come on Van, you know me better than that. Of course it's real. I worked my ass off for it, but it's worth it. All nice things come with a price."

"That's for sure," I responded. "It's so good to see you."

For a few minutes all seemed normal once again. His company was the best. He could always make me laugh, no matter how horrible a day I'd had.

As we sat next to each other, huddled underneath the blanket, I felt his hand slide into mine. I tried my hardest not to act surprised, but I was surprised. And I liked his hand there.

Anyhow, we talked about a lot, about how things were going with me, and how Elijah's new-found work was going. He told me that he'd worked almost every day for those last three weeks, including daytime hours. I was a little upset because he'd skipped school for an entire week. He tried his best to assure me that it was okay, and he wouldn't fail. I tried to believe him, even though I knew that school was not his priority. In his mind he thought that because he was making good money, why should he worry about school? I really wanted him to finish, but it wasn't my choice.

"Oh yeah, I almost forgot," he said abruptly, reaching into his pocket. "I have something for you."

He pulled out a wad of cash from his pocket, and went through it for a moment, counting out hundreds. He ended up giving me a couple of hundred, which I tried to hand back to him.

"Elijah, I can't take that from you."

"Oh come on, why not? I know you need it. And besides, there's more where that came from," he laughed.

"I don't know. I don't think it would be right of me, ya know?"

"It's no biggie," he said, shoving the wad of cash back into his pocket. "Go get yourself some new clothes or somethin', or umm – take a shower?"

"Ha ha, very funny," I said, accepting the money. "I feel bad, though."

"No problem, really. Don't go thinkin' I'm gonna be doing that all the time though," he smiled.

I couldn't believe he gave me that much money. Don't get me wrong – I appreciated it, I was just surprised. I didn't want him to think that because he was making good money, he had to support me.

It was then that it started.

"One other thing," he said. "We need to celebrate."

"Celebrate what?"

"Me, of course."

"You?"

"Yeah. Celebrate how well I am doing – thanks to my girl," he smirks.

"Whatcha wanna do? We should have lunch. You know I'm all about the grub!" I laughed.

"I brought something," he started. "Before I show you, though, just know that it will be okay. I've had a few personal treats, and it was never noticed. A little bit won't hurt."

"What are you talking about?"

Elijah reached into the pocket on his sweatshirt and pulled it out, a small zip-lock bag filled with white powder.

"This," he said, holding the bag for me to see.

"I don't know about that, Jah. What is it? Coke?"

"Nah, nah – it's meth. It's all good though, Van. One time isn't gonna getcha hooked, and it's an awesome feeling."

"You tried it?"

"Yeah. I was bored one night while I was out working near 26th Street."

"If Jon knew that, he would be pissed! You better be careful with that, ya know?"

"He's not gonna find out, it's only a little. And besides, that dude loves me."

"Not enough to let you take money from him," I joked.

"It'll be okay."

"I guess."

The tiny bag was packed tight and filled to the brim with powder. I was nervous. I wasn't sure how I felt about it, but I didn't think one time would hurt.

I watched him intently as he placed the bag between his legs. His eyes were fixed, trying to keep the bag level. He reached into his pocket and pulled out a tiny mirror.

"Hold that for a sec," he said.

Silently I sat there and watched what he was doing. I had to hold back, fighting the giggles about to escape my lips, as he reached his hand inside the bag and picked up a little of the powder. I remembered watching some things on television about cocaine, so I thought he was going to do something elaborate or sophisticated – instead he used his hand. He put a pinch of powder on top of the mirror, separating it with a small rusted razor blade, and then lined it up.

To me, it didn't look like a lot, so I trusted his judgment that it would be okay. I couldn't imagine Jon noticing that it was gone, or anyone else for that matter.

"Ready?" Elijah began.

"I guess so. How do you do it?"

"It's simple. Watch."

He pulled out a dollar bill, rolled it tightly, as if it were a straw, and held it over the powder-covered mirror. He glanced over at me and smiled before deeply inhaling the powder through his nose. Quickly, the line was gone.

"Damn! All of it? Isn't that too much?" I asked.

"Nah, that's a normal amount."

Elijah reached into his bag and grabbed a little more of the powder, placing it on top of the mirror. He lined it up quickly and handed me the rolled bill.

"Use it like you would a straw."

I sat there and looked at the powder. It was all new to me then, so the thought of snorting that stuff up my nose made me nervous. But instead of asking any more questions, I leaned down and took all of it in.

My nose immediately itched in an unfamiliar and peculiar way. My body still felt normal, but then again I wasn't exactly sure of what I was supposed to be feeling.

"How long does it take to hit?"

"Just lay back and relax. It will only take a few minutes."

After that, Elijah and I laid next to each other, silently. He lit a cigarette, then once again placed his hand in mine. My mind started to drift, and a smile came upon my face as my body began to relax.

That was the first time I'd felt completely and thoroughly happy. I remember, even at that moment, wanting to feel like that every day. That was the beginning of my journey with meth.

I come awake in the alley, not panicked, but disoriented. My head is pounding, but at least my shakiness has subsided. I don't remember feeling as upset as I was earlier for a long time. It's like my own memories are stalking me.

It's pitch black outside and I'm late for work. It's the last thing I want to do right now; I'd rather sit here and sleep, but

I'm broke. I need cash for food tomorrow, and maybe I can get my hands on some meth. I'm sure it won't be that hard to find someone who can give me a bag, even if it's only twenty dollars worth. I need it.

My mind is starting to drive me insane.

CHAPTER 9

It's 4:20 in the morning.

I just woke up. I am lying on a cruddy motel room floor. My vision is foggy and I have the worst headache, more painful than any headache I have ever experienced. I'm a little disoriented and feel like I have been asleep for days, but judging by the alarm clock on the nightstand it has only been about an hour.

My night started off okay, I guess. I had a nose bleed that lasted for about two hours, so until it stopped I walked up and down Benz Street with a tissue plugged in my nose. Needless to say, the nose bleed made it difficult for any man to find me appealing. But when it dried and I managed to wipe the blood off my face, the men rolled in, one after another.

I was picked up by a few different men, one of them being a regular. The first two weren't so bad. Like I said before, what I do disgusts me, but they were pretty well mannered and didn't treat me like a piece of garbage.

The second pick up was a quick job. We stayed in his car the entire time. He didn't talk much, either – just drove around while I did what he asked. Gross.

My third and last client of the night was the asshole who left me in the state I'm in now, in this mess of a motel room. It was maybe two hours ago when this nasty man picked me up. When he pulled up next to me I had a gut feeling that he was a weirdo, and I should've followed my instincts. But instead I thought about the money. It's too late for that now.

He had a nice car, a Mercedes SUV to be exact. Normally I would think a nice car like that would hold a decent person, but not this time. When I say decent, I mean more normal than most of the men that stalk this side of town.

Anyway, in his own way he was attractive. He was clean shaven, his hair was spiked in the front, and he was wearing a designer silk suit. Why he was dressed like that at 2am is beyond me, but he was.

From the moment he began talking to me I had a feeling that he was not a person that I wanted to be alone with. He was talking about some freaky stuff, like chains, whips and blindfolds. That is not my thing at all. Judging by his wedding ring, it's not his wife's thing either – that's why he was out on the street looking for it.

It's obvious that I decided to join him, because I'm lying here on this dirty floor. I shouldn't have got into his car, but I did. I couldn't resist the couple of hundred dollars that he was offering. I have never been given that much money by one person. Hell, I am lucky if I make that much from one night's work. On most nights I only manage to make thirty to forty dollars, which is nothing. That small amount of cash used to take me a lot further – before I started using – but now it's enough to grab a bite to eat and a pack of cigarettes. After that, I have a few more bills to spare that I could use for something else – but I need to save as much as I can. Like I said, Elijah used to be my supplier; he would give me meth for absolutely nothing. Now that he's gone, I need to pay my own way.

Once I got into his car he immediately sped off. The interior was as immaculate as the outside of the car. It was fully loaded with XM Radio, a DVD player and leather seats. I tried not to look around, because I didn't want to make him suspicious of me in any way, but I did manage to spot a small duffle bag on his back seat. That is where the horrendous night began.

He drove me to a motel fifteen minutes away from Benz Street – a motel I didn't even know existed. I remember thinking that I had no idea where we were, and for the first time in a while I felt lost out there on the street.

The inside of the motel was like any other ratty motel in the area – dirty. The carpet and bed linen probably hadn't been cleaned for a while, as well as the toilet seat in the bathroom – it was covered with urine stains. The smell of stale smoke consumed the room and the lighting was dim, immediately giving the place a miserable feeling.

I couldn't understand why a man like him, obviously full of money, would want to stay in a room like that. I mean, he could afford better – at least a hotel that kept a maid service on duty every day. But perhaps he wanted a mangled room for his odd fetishes, or maybe he didn't think a better one would suit a girl like me. All the same, it didn't make sense.

Once in the room, he simultaneously took off his jacket and collared shirt, and threw the duffle bag onto the bed. I stood there watching him as he silently dug through the bag. Normally I would be the one to take action, but this was completely different. I had no idea what to say or do.

Silently, he motioned for me to sit on the bed. His gaze was suddenly terrifying, especially when a smirk appeared upon his face. It reminded me of stinky Johnny, immediately bringing a nauseating feeling to the surface.

He pulled out a weird piece of lingerie and handed it to me. Without asking any questions, I quickly took off my clothes and put it on, at the same time trying to settle my stomach. There wasn't any talking going on between him and me, which disturbed me. He just motioned with his hands, indicating to me what he wanted me to do.

The night got even weirder when he took out a blindfold and a small whip. I wasn't sure who was going to use it and that made me nervous, because surely I didn't want to get beaten with that thing. My nerves calmed a little though when he put the red satin blindfold on himself. I figured I would be smacking him, which didn't bother me as much as the alternative.

To cut a long story short, the first twenty minutes were okay. He did have me whip him, which truly wasn't that bad. At first I was uncomfortable, but after a few minutes I swung that thing against his skin like I was taming a horse. The way he enjoyed it made me feel queasy. His sick yelps and moans each time I hit him was the worst part. I kept thinking – what am I doing? Money talks though, and I couldn't pass up two hundred dollars.

When he said he was finished I thought my job with him was done – oh, how wrong I was! The smile on his face revealed how pleased he was. I couldn't understand it. He didn't even seem to mind that his back was bleeding. Anyway, he took the bandana off and immediately tied it around my head. I didn't like that.

"What are you doing?" I asked, trying not to sound panicky.

I tried to take the bandana off, but couldn't. He didn't acknowledge my question, just grabbed my arms and pulled them out from underneath me. I couldn't get away from him, or even get off the bed. Within seconds, my arms were tied to the bedpost, and my legs did their own thing as I kicked the air hoping to reach his face. All the time, he never said a word.

I tried everything to get my arms out of the knotted rope, but couldn't. I tried to use my voice before something bad happened. It didn't work.

"Please, let me go. I did what you asked and I really need to get back."

"Not yet," is all he said to me. The first words he'd spoken since we'd got to the motel.

I squirmed and I yelled, and he got mad. Suddenly, I felt something smash against my face. I'm not sure if it was his fist, but it definitely was his hand, and it hurt – bad. Right away, my right eye started to swell. There was second blow to my head, and another. I begged for him to stop, but he didn't care.

He smacked me around for at least ten minutes, although it felt like hours.

By the time he was finished, or I thought he was finished, I felt like I had been hit by a truck. I couldn't see anything, I could hear him standing above me, panting like a dog. I was crying silently under the blindfold, praying that the night would end.

After that, the rest of the night was a blur. I know that he raped and beat me no end. I know that people would think that saying rape is probably crazy considering my job, but I did tell him to get off me, and he didn't listen. I have never had that happen since I've been out here on the street. I can't believe I got into his car, either – that was stupid. Money rules the world. And I'm more naïve than I realised.

I am still lying on the floor, unsure of how I got here, next to the window. I'm still shaken up about what happened, and my anxiety level has shot through the roof. It's difficult to steady my hands, and my head is killing me. At least my vision has cleared a little, allowing me to see my surroundings.

The room is in a bad condition, worse than how it was when we first got here. The bed is a mess, blood is covering the sheets.

I have finally managed to stand up, but I have to hold onto the nightstand just in case I become wobbly and lose my balance.

I try to avoid vomiting as I search the room for my clothes. After five minutes, I find them, extremely wrinkled and rolled into a ball, in the corner by the dirty bathroom.

Strategically placed next to my clothes are the blindfold and rope. He must have placed them there, the asshole. I can't find my money anywhere. Not only did he beat and rape me, he left me here without even paying what he'd promised.

It goes through my mind that he could've killed me. I really think that if he'd kept on going, it would have happened. He managed to beat me unconscious – so death wasn't too far away.

My memory searches for Elijah's comforting eyes. I can't stop crying. I don't know whether it's because my head hurts so badly, or if I'm going through withdrawal, or if I just miss Elijah that much.

Without him, my days only seem to get worse. Maybe tonight's events wouldn't have happened if he was still around. I know he wasn't my protector, but emotionally he gave me a lot. With his friendship I didn't feel so alone or helpless. Without it, I don't seem to care about anything at all. Maybe this is who I am. Maybe this life is all that's left for me.

Why, Elijah? Why did you have to go?

CHAPTER 10

When I left the cruddy motel I was still hidden in the darkness of night, hidden from any passers-by who might stop and stare. Not now. The sun is slowly beginning to peak out over the cityscape, forcing a spotlight to beam down upon my face. I wish I was invisible, not existing to any of the people who are walking the streets this early in the morning. But I am not, and they continue to stare.

I feel like I've already walked ten miles, but it's probably only been one. What's worse than the distance is my lack of balance and the loose pieces of gravel digging into my bare feet. Yeah, I had shoes, but I decided to leave them behind. The heel on one snapped, so what's the use in trying to wear them? They would look even more hideous than they did before.

Ever since I woke up from the floor of that disgusting motel room, I've felt unsteady and disoriented. I took a quick shower but even that didn't help. Well, it washed away some of the grime that was caked onto my body, just not the dried blood on my face. I tried to scrub, but it hurt too much. There was no way I wanted the cuts on my forehead to reopen, so I gently washed around them.

The street isn't too busy this early in the morning, but on this side of town the rich folk come out to do their fitness routines. There is a park behind the boutiques, made for jogging, biking or rollerblading, so I try to stay out of the way as young men and women jog by dressed in designer workout clothing, iPods attached to their arms. It doesn't seem to work, though – I can feel their eyes on me, staring at me. Just because they have a perfect life full of riches, why do they have to look at me that way? Idiots.

With my head in a daze it's hard, but I try to concentrate, focusing on the ground as I walk. I feel like I might fall over at any moment, swaying from side to side as if I were a drunk. I start to perspire and my tattered clothes begin to cling to my body. I feel like I could vomit. I have a long way to go, though, walking next to these damn boutiques. I'm sure the owners won't let me in to use the restrooms. My appearance alone is enough to isolate me from what most people call a 'normal' world.

Maybe that's what I need – a fix. I have enough left in my bag for a handful of lines and it could only make me feel better, right? It has to, because right now I feel like I could fall over and die. But where? There isn't anywhere for me to go. I have to keep moving forward, out of this place, away from the eyes of these have-it-all, good-for-nothing rich people.

In front of the fine jewelry store I stumble and fall to the ground. My hands break my fall, but I land on broken glass. I try to hold it in, but I can't.

"Dammit!" I scream. I look at the palm of my hand and a tiny piece of glass is sticking out of my skin. I sit on the tarmac and tremble as I try to pull out the glass. My hands hurt so badly that I don't pay any attention to the young woman approaching. "Shit!" I yell, pulling out as much of the glass as I can.

"Are you okay?" the woman asks. She startles me.

"I'm fine," I respond, standing up and distancing myself from her.

I try to walk away from her, but she grabs my arm.

"Are you okay sweetie? Do you need help?"

"Get off of me!" I yell. She does.

She might have been trying to help, but she didn't have to grab me. Besides, she probably just wanted to make a good impression to all the other rich idiots out here watching. That's right, watching me. I hate that. I hate them. I wish they would all go away.

I feel it now. My anxiety is rising and I feel angry. My stomach hurts even worse than it did before. I can't hold it in and vomit escapes my mouth. I try to push it back in, but it only seeps through my fingers, landing on my already disgusting shirt. Now there are even more eyes staring at me, more comments from those passing. What is their problem?

"What the hell are all of you looking at?" I yell, circling, looking at every one of them. "I don't feel good, what's the big deal? Mind your own business, you rich idiots!"

I try to run, stumbling yet managing to stay on my feet. I don't know where I am going exactly, because I'm not so sure where I am or which route to take to get back to my bridge. Screw it, though. I just need to get out of here.

Tears fall, even when it's anger that is brewing inside me. I'm angry at myself, at these streets – but most of all, at Elijah. Why did he have to go? Why did he have to be so stupid? He could've been great as a normal person, having a normal life. Too late now. He's gone.

I don't want to, but I see his face flashing before my eyes. He's not handsome anymore, though – he is covered in blood. He wants me to help him, but it's too late.

"Get out of my head!" I yell.

I don't want to see him like that. I want to remember how he used to be, not how he was after what they did to him. Not like that. I can't push him away; he is still there staring at me, trying to smile as blood drips off his forehead like sweat. Please let me forget. But I can't forget, and maybe that's because I don't deserve to forget.

The afternoon had been horrible that day, when it all went wrong. It was freezing cold outside and pouring with rain. I remember feeling miserable the entire day, even before I met Elijah. I didn't want to do anything other than sleep or get high.

After work, I'd immediately gone back to my bridge to rest. I was hungry, but didn't care about food – I was too tired. I also wanted to take in my last line before sleeping and seeing Elijah. I knew he was going to be giving me a brand new bag, so one line would surely hold me over until then.

There was nothing out of the ordinary about that morning. It was quiet, boring and monotonous. I didn't expect anything more of the afternoon, even though Elijah and I were going to hang out. I thought it was going to be just the same as it always was. I was wrong – dead wrong.

Anyway, I met Elijah at a sandwich shop near Benz Street around noon. I was excited to see him. With all that was going on in his life we didn't get to see each other so often now. When we did, it was only for thirty minutes here or there, so not nearly enough time to progress our relationship. I'd thought about it for days, and then finally I'd decided that it was going to be today day when I asked. I had to know if he wanted us to be a couple. I hoped he would.

We spent nearly an hour in the shop that day, eating, talking and joking around. It felt good to hear his voice, his laugh and all about his work with Jon. He still felt confident, having no worries when it came to how he handled his business.

Towards the end of our lunch I mentioned my feelings to him. I felt, like, self-conscious for a minute, stuttering and fumbling over my words, but it all turned out okay.

"Can I ask you something?" I asked before we stood up to leave.

"Sure, Van, what's up?"

I felt my face turn red. Suddenly I was shy – something I never usually was around Elijah.

"Um, I don't know," I giggled, "I guess I was just wondering if maybe, uh–"

"Yes," he said before I could even finish. He laughed, and then grabbed my hand. "You don't have to say anymore. I know," he smiled.

"Do ya?" I managed to say.

"You know I been all about you, Van, for a while."

I didn't respond, just smiled back at him as he rubbed my hand with his finger. I felt butterflies in my stomach and wanted to kiss him. I wanted to tell him everything I was feeling, but thought it was best to leave it at that moment. I wish I hadn't. I wish I'd told him that I loved him.

Ten minutes later, that beautiful moment between us was shattered into pieces.

Once we left the shop we walked together to the park, where we were going to go our separate ways. On the way, we spoke about little things, nothing huge – just our lives and where we wanted to go. He had big plans; I wanted eventually to escape my life and become a little more normal.

I felt bad when he handed me the bag of meth. I had mixed feelings. I didn't want to just take it from him, but I needed it. He assured me that no one was noticing the amounts he was taking for his pleasure. We both agreed that after that bag was gone, we would stop using.

Anyway, the street was silent and appeared to be abandoned. There was no one outside on that block, not even kids playing on their bikes. Granted, it was the ghetto area, but it was too quiet, even for there. Chills went down my spine as our steps echoed against the exterior of the residential homes.

The chills I was feeling were a sign that I shouldn't have ignored. Within seconds

Elijah was laying on the cobblestone street screaming in pain. A group of four boys, huge boys, gathered around him and set about beating him with chains and a bat. As they took turns striking his body, I tried to get them to stop – but they pushed me away every time, threatening me with the bat.

Suddenly, Elijah's screams stopped. He lay there, motionless, with blood oozing from his head. I was frozen and couldn't move. I couldn't scream either. I was too scared. Why would they do that? Why? I wanted to grab Elijah and pull him out of the street, kiss his forehead – but I couldn't. They were still standing there.

One of the guys was looking at me, pointing his blood-drenched bat in my direction.

"You better get lost, trick," he announced, walking towards me and threatening that I would be next.

I tried to run, turning my back on my best friend. As I ran off I heard one last smash against his body.

"That's from Jon. Never forget it, punk!"

I started to cry immediately. Without even thinking twice, I knew those kids had just beaten Elijah to death. I stopped running but didn't dare turn around, even though I badly wanted to.

If I'd walked up to Elijah at that very moment, I would have been dead too.

What if he wasn't dead when they were finished with him? I left him there all alone, taking a bath in his own blood...

This is why his vision haunts me.

CHAPTER 11

I wake up with the stench of vomit in my nostrils, in an alleyway near one of the fancy boutiques. I'm not really sure how I got here, I can't remember. But here I am, leaning against a brick wall, still shaking uncontrollably. My eyes are almost swollen shut from all the crying and my throat hurts. I'm a bloody mess, but I don't really care.

I know I made a fool of myself earlier, walking down the street next to those rich people, but it's like I can't control myself anymore. Unless I'm high. That is what I need to do right now, take in a few lines.

I need to get out of this rut and I need to stop thinking about Elijah. I can still see his face, his lips motioning silently for help. Dammit.

I wouldn't normally pull out a bag and sniff a line or two in plain daylight, especially on this side of town – but I need it. Two or three lines won't hurt, and I will be on my way. I can't rest here. I will rest when I get back to my spot by Flannigan's.

I sit back for a few moments, waiting for the feeling to hit and rush through my body. I know it's only temporary, but the blissful numbing sensation is what I need right now – and to get out of this uppity neighborhood, away from the ridiculing eyes.

A half-hour has passed and I'm still walking – but I'm close to home. I decided to walk behind the buildings, instead of on the sidewalk next to all the morning shoppers. It's better this way.

The block I am passing now is still considered to be part of the wealthy area. Even the backs of the boutiques are fancy – the dumpsters are clean, and there isn't any trash to be seen anywhere. It's spotless. The workers have sitting areas in the back, with fancy chairs and tables for them to sit at on their lunch breaks.

The transition between the rich side of town and the poor is quite funny. In front of me, within only a few feet, the change is apparent. Trash is overflowing from the dumpsters and the area is not even slightly clean or spotless. Often enough, teenagers from this area hang out behind the stores at night, drinking and smoking marijuana. From the looks of things I'm guessing that they throw out their empty malt liquor bottles when they are finished – but not in the trash. There is broken glass all over the tarmac.

It's odd; my stomach is growling and I know that I'm hungry, but I don't feel like eating. I feel sick, and my perspiration is only getting worse now that my buzz has nearly worn off. Inside I am trembling, for whatever reason; I could jump out of my own skin. I need more. I need a few more lines to carry me.

Benz Street is a few blocks away, so I'm nearly there. I can't wait until then, though. There is a little park, although it's normally gang-infested, just another block up. There isn't any playground equipment or anything, just a few picnic tables. If it's not occupied by anyone, especially Jon's boys, I will sit there for a few minutes and get my fix.

Luckily, the park is abandoned at this hour. Everyone is probably still asleep, hung over from a night of drugging and partying. There is a table underneath a lone tree, which will be the perfect spot for me. It will keep me hidden from anyone who might pass by.

My bag is nearly empty. I might as well finish it off while I'm here. Maybe my high will last a little longer.

The wooden table is completely worn out and infested with termites. It doesn't matter, though. The flat surface will make it easier to take in a few lines.

I was going to be careful about it, make sure not to drop any of it onto the ground – but screw it. I pour the remaining amount into the palm of my hand, losing only a tiny bit to the mud-covered floor. With my fingers, I strategically separate the powder into six lines. There is more left than I thought. That will surely prolong my high.

Within thirty seconds I take in all six lines, leaving only a little residue on the table. I cover my face with my trembling hands and rest my elbows on the table, until I feel the drug rushing through my body.

This time it's different. Inside I feel more relaxed, but my body is still shaking, trembling. If I don't lie down on the table for a moment I might fall to the ground. I can't stand up, and my eyes are twitching uncontrollably.

I've lost all control. I can feel myself lying here, but cannot move.

I fall deep into a dream-like state. I can't fight it, even though I try. And it's like I'm taken somewhere else, somewhere that is not here, not in this park.

Wherever I am, this place has a musty smell to it, along with the scent of cigar smoke and mothballs. The lighting is dim, but I manage to see three large shadows against the wood-panelled wall. The men aren't in the room with me, though – I don't think. They are cackling with one another in the adjoining room, hacking and coughing fit to bring up a lung.

I can't make out what they are saying and don't want to find out either – what if they don't know I'm here?

A Forgotten Tomorrow

Something, maybe dust, flies into my nose without warning, bringing forth a loud sneeze. I cover my mouth, trying to force back another that is on its way. It's too late. The large men must have already heard me, because their cackling abruptly stops. There is silence.

I realise that I'm backed into a corner. I've been here the entire time, not realising it until now. My arms are tied behind my back and my cry is muffled by a gag that's in my mouth. What's going on? Oh my God! Here they come.

The man that appears in front of my face is very unclean and extremely large. His tank top looks ten years old. At one point it was probably white, but not anymore. It's covered with stains, most likely because of his nasty perspiration – he reeks of body odor. His long, tangled beard covers most of his mouth, but when he smiles I notice that he is missing a lot of his teeth. Those that remain appear to be rotted, judging by his breath, which smells like halitosis.

His long, chubby arms reach down towards my face. What is he doing? I can't move. I can't scream. Leave me alone! I feel his grip on my shoulder. I try to shrug him away, but cannot move...

I convulse, shake and vomit uncontrollably. I don't think I'm dreaming any more, but still cannot move. My eyes are fluttering. I can't see anything of my surroundings, but briefly I notice a man standing above me.

He looks exactly like the man I just saw in my dream – with no teeth. He appears to be upset. Why does he keep shaking me?

"Hang on. I'm gonna call an ambulance," he says.

I can barely understand what he's saying. Everything is muffled and unclear.

I don't want an ambulance. Why would he be doing that? I'm okay. I'm just resting for a minute, dude...

Everything is black. My body is convulsing, yet I feel completely numb. There is silence. What's happening?

CHAPTER 12

It's pitch black.

I can't open my eyes, nor can I move. My body feels paralysed and the sound of people chattering in the distance is starting to make my skin crawl. I can't see them. Where am I? What is that beeping sound and why is my mouth so sore? Can anyone hear me?

I try to force my eyes open and after much effort I can see, but with fuzzy vision. I'm in a white room, surrounded by an odd-looking curtain and stainless steel cabinets.

There is an overwhelming smell of surgical alcohol too. I start to gag. My hands are strapped to a gurney so I can't sit up.

"Help!" I scream as loud as I possibly can without gagging and vomiting all over the blue gown that I'm wearing. "Get me outta this room!"

Two female nurses dressed in light blue surgical scrubs run into my room quickly. One of them is young, in her mid-twenties maybe. The other looks like she is fifty at best. They don't say much at first, but they are calm and attentive.

"What the hell is going on?" I ask, still gagging and mildly panicking.

"Calm down, calm down. You're at County Hospital," the older nurse says.

"What? Why?"

"You overdosed."

"On what?" I cough, gag. "I want to sit up. I can't move my arms."

"Try to relax." She tries to reassure me.

I'm panicking, but at least they untie my hands. "What's this?" I ask the young nurse, pointing to the bandage wrapped around my head.

"What's your name?" she asks.

"Savannah."

"Well, Savannah, did you get into a fight or something?"

"You could say that," I mumble, trying to speak through the pain that's burning down my throat.

"We had to give you some stitches. You had some pretty bad cuts on your forehead."

I feel nauseous and try to force it back, but I can't help it. I throw up all over the gurney and on the younger nurse who's next to me.

"Feel better?" she asks, trying to stay calm. If I were her I'd be out of here by now, taking a shower.

I nod my head in silence. I do feel better, but I also feel kind of bad that I puked on the woman.

"I'll bring you a clean gown," she says. And with that, they both leave the room.

They forgot to close my curtain. They left it wide open for everyone to peek in, and I can't handle that. I have to close it.

My only intention as I reach the curtain is to close it, but what I see when I get closer makes me nervous. The nurse's station is probably about ten feet from my room, making it easy to eavesdrop on the current conversations – and to notice that there is a man with a badge talking with the two

nurses who were just in my room. He'd
better not be here for me. I can't stay here
and I definitely cannot go to jail.

"No it's not cocaine, it's meth we found
in her system," the older nurse says to the
policeman. A moment passes before she
continues, "We need to ask her about her
family first, since she's under age."

I panic, quickly getting back on the
gurney. I can't leave right now, I don't have
any clothes, and if that man wants to take
me away I'll be in even more trouble than I
am now. And what's that about my family?
There is no way I am going back to Mama –
I never want to see her again. I'd rather rot.
I feel crazy. I'm scared, really scared and I
don't know what to do.

Minutes later, the young nurse enters
the room, interrupting my irrational plan
to escape. She is carrying a sweat suit in
her hands, and she places it on my lap.

"This is from the share box downstairs. I figured you might want some proper clothing to change into."

"Where's my stuff?" I ask.

"We had to throw it away," she responds, looking directly into my eyes. "Before you change, I need to ask you a couple questions though."

I don't like the sound of that, and neither does my stomach. I feel sick.

"What?" I hesitantly ask.

"It's not a lot, just a few questions that we need to ask before we let you go."

"I can leave?"

"Shortly. But we can't let you leave alone. Do you have anyone you can call – family? Relatives?"

I'm nervous, but I can't cry or scream – all I can do is laugh. It's not a normal laugh either. I probably sound crazy to this woman. Oh well. "I don't have any family," I finally say.

"None?"

"Nope."

"Hmm," she starts, "Well, we can't let you walk out of here without your guardian, and if you don't have anyone, there is an officer out there who will be taking you with him."

"What?" I ask, louder than I intended. "Why?"

"Considering why you are here, we can't just let you go without a treatment plan."

"Well what am I supposed to do?" I yell. Tears are beginning to fill my eyes. "I don't have a damn family!"

"Where are you from, Savannah?"

"Under a rock."

"Under a rock?" she asks. "Where is your mother?"

"I don't have one! Can't you just leave me alone?"

"I'm sorry to upset you, but we need to have some more information. Either you tell me, or talk to that nice officer outside your room."

They're flowing now, my tears. My stomach is turning and my anxiety level is increasing every moment. I can't stop my hands from shaking, or my entire body for that matter. Rocking will help. I need to rock myself back and forth. This isn't happening.

"I – I don't know," I cry. "I don't wanna talk to him, I just want to leave. Why can't I just leave?"

"I'm sorry sweetie, but you need some help." She tries to comfort me, but I don't let her. I don't want her near me. She's looking at me all funny too – they are all judging me, laughing on the inside, I just know it.

I rock myself, tears falling, odd noises escaping from my mouth. It's a cry, a loud and uncontrollable cry that has been waiting for the right time to surface. I feel more alone than I ever have. I feel vulnerable and forgotten. I don't have a family, I don't have anyone. I did have Elijah, but he was the only person in my life I could count on. So how the hell am I going to get out of here if I don't have anyone to call? I don't want to go with that man.

"You have some time, okay Savannah?" the nurse continues. "Get dressed and sit here for a little bit, maybe something will come to mind. I'll be back in twenty minutes."

She touches my arm, trying to comfort me. I don't respond. I sit in this same spot, rocking.

Minutes pass before I can even think about anything, or calm down. All I can do after she leaves is cry. I feel a little calmer now, but I'm still scared because I can't figure out how I'm going to get out of here. Who can I call?

I think harder and harder, trying to find a solution. I've been on these streets for over a year, with little to no contact with the normal, outside world. I can't call my old case worker because I'd be sent back to yet another hell-hole, with another crazy foster parent. No way.

Finally – I've got it. As much as I don't want to, maybe I can call Jonah. After the way I acted towards him he might not want anything to do with me, but I can try. He probably would help me get out of here, if he's truly all about helping kids like me. Honestly, if he does pick me up though, I don't plan on staying. I don't think so anyway. I will use him to break out of this damn hospital, and once I'm in the clear – I'm running.

That's it. I will call Jonah.

CHAPTER 13

The pale white wall of this hospital room is about as comforting as Jonah's office. I hate sitting here waiting. I'd rather just leave – but I can't. There are a dozen or more doctors and nurses outside, carrying on with their daily routine. As well as that stupid policeman who is still standing at the nurse's station, waiting to see what's going to happen with me.

I finally speak to the younger nurse and tell her about Jonah and the City Community Center. He's the only one I could think of to get me out of here – the only other person I have really talked to, except for Elijah, during my time in this forsaken city. It works, though. She calls him and he agrees to come by to talk with me. Great.

I don't know what's taking him so long. It's been at least a couple of hours since she called him. It's not like the Center is that far away from here. He could walk it in five or ten minutes if he wanted to.

I can't say I'm looking forward to seeing him, either. I mean, I look like I just got run over by a truck, and by now I'm sure this entire hospital has heard about me — the overdosed junky prostitute. That's not who I am. Who's to say that I overdosed anyway? Thanks to that insane client, I was already a mess before I got here. It could have simply been the after-effects of him beating me. Whatever.

Here comes Jonah. He hasn't entered my room, but I can see his face through the small opening of the curtain. He's at the nurses station talking to someone. I don't know who, all I can see is a finger pointing in my direction. That same compassionate look is still on his face. Does anyone else think that that's weird, I wonder? Who walks around smiling and looking like that every day? I've never known anyone else to, but then again, who am I? No one.

Jonah opens the curtain at last, peeking in before entering. "Savannah?"

"Uh-huh," I respond. He knows I'm in here. That nurse just told him. So why didn't he just walk in? Again, I swear he's nuts. But if he can get me out of here, I don't care if he has schizophrenia.

"Glad to see you again, although not in these circumstances," he says, as he pulls up a stool next to the gurney. "I was sure you'd forgotten about me. I guess some things happen for a reason, and I'm glad you changed your mind."

"Can you just get me out of here?"

"Well, we need to talk about a few things first. I can probably get the police officer and nurses outside to let you come with me, but we need a plan of action."

"What do you mean?" I ask. A plan of action? Why would we need that? Just get me out of this room! It's making me crazy.

"In order to take you with me, you will have to agree to take any assistance I can give you — whatever that may be. And I will have to let the authorities know." He stops talking for a minute, waiting for my response, but I have nothing to say.

I guess things aren't going to be that easy — me just walking out of here and getting back to my life, I mean. I don't know if I want to stay with Jonah. Either way I'm a lost cause, up the creek without a paddle. I'm lost to this world of chaos, stuck in this city of harm. Who is Jonah anyway? Not God, that's for sure.

"How old are you again? Sixteen, you said?"

"Yup."

"I see. Well, that's why we would need to have this agreement with the proper authorities."

"Why?"

"Technically you are still a minor, but because you have been out here alone for more than a year, we can probably make a court appearance and have you cleared as an adult – after you receive proper treatment."

"What kinda treatment?"

"First? Rehab."

"Hell no! I'm not going to rehab. I'm not crazy! You think I'm crazy!" I begin to yell. Tears begin to fall from my eyes. I wish they would stop and I wish my hands would stop shaking.

"I don't think you are crazy, Savannah. Rehab is for people who need help," he replies rather calmly. "After rehab, which lasts for three months, we can then begin to talk about the next step."

"Three months?" I cry.

"Yes. But really, in terms of the life you have ahead of you, three months isn't that long."

"What happens after that? I don't know if I can do this."

"After rehab I would find you a placement, where you will have the opportunity to get a job in the community, and finish school if you'd like. It's your decision. But rehab is required."

Is he joking? I don't need rehab. I can stop using any time I please. He has to be full of it, all this stuff he's promising. I'd be better off with that damn police officer out there. I'm a minor; how much time would I get? A month? A month in jail would be a lot easier than three months in rehab and everything else Jonah is talking about. I'm not cut out for a normal life. I'm comfortable right now with my life. How the hell can I start over, just like that? It's too much.

I can hear Jonah's voice, but I'm not listening to a word he is saying. My imagination takes me to the distant future, twenty years from this very day. It's an odd feeling, staring at myself when I'm thirty-five or thirty-six years old. That woman doesn't look like me either, but I know that she is. She hasn't aged well; she looks about fifty. The skin on her throat is dangling like a chicken's, and her skin is very dark and rough in appearance. Judging by her sunken eyes she's a junkie too – probably a heroin addict.

She's wearing a short denim mini skirt and a low cut tank top – not very appealing at all. Her legs are scrawny. She is too thin all around – I can see her ribs from a distance, even. That woman's hair is thinning way too quickly for her age; it's probably falling out due to drug abuse.

Even then, twenty years from now, Benz Street looks the same at night. The ladies of work, the prostitutes, are still prancing around the sidewalks looking for their next trick. This woman – me in twenty years' time – appears to be working too much. I surely hope she has been safe, protecting herself from the various diseases that can be caught in an instant, working the streets.

I know I would always protect myself. I wouldn't be so stupid, and surely I would never shoot up heroin! I hate needles. So that vision cannot be true. Why would I even imagine such a thing?

I would never.

Within moments, even with Jonah's constant chattering, my mind goes to another distant place, but one that's very unfamiliar.

It's twenty years later again, but now I'm at a school playground. Tons of kids are running around, chasing one another and sliding down large, plastic slides. They are younger children, grade school probably, and as cute as can be.

I'm standing next to the entrance doors of the school, with a whistle around my neck. Am I a teacher? And wow, I'm beautiful. That can't possibly be me. She surely looks like me though, except she's older and is wearing a gorgeous dress, with chucky heels. The dress is gently swaying in the wind. I don't ever remember the sky being such a perfect shade of blue.

Her hair is long and straight, and incredibly shiny. She could probably star in one of those Pantene commercials. Anyway, her smile is amazing too. She seems genuinely happy.

After staring at her for a moment, I have this warm sensation inside. I would have never thought I could look like her, or someone like her.

Could that really be me in twenty years? There's no way. The junkie seems to be more of who I am now. But can I change? I doubt it, not like that.

I only come back to reality because Jonah claps his hands in front of my face. I have no idea what he has been talking about, and my blank stare proves it.

"Are you okay?" he asks.

"Uh, yeah I guess."

"Where'd ya go?"

"Nowhere – just spaced out for a minute," I respond.

"So, what do you think?"

About what? I don't even know what you were saying, and I don't know if I want to leave with you. I can't answer that right now; that's a huge deal.

Can I move on, beyond this crazy city? I'm not sure I have what it takes. Maybe I was meant to live this life of struggling. Not everyone is dealt a fair hand, with a life of luxury and kindness to enjoy. Some people are born into a world of harm, drugs, corruption, prostitution and murder. Sad, but true. It's the only world that has ever welcomed me with open arms, whether I was born into it or not. Like I said, I'm one of the forgotten ones. So, do I have a chance at a better life? Who knows.

"I need a few minutes to sort some things out," I say to Jonah. And that's what I'm doing. I'm taking time to think. I need to be sure that I'm making the right decision.

I've been shown two visions of a possible future. You'd think that it would be a no-brainer; that I should go with Jonah and follow the path that leads to me becoming that beautiful, confident, fulfilled woman. But it's not that simple. I'm not sure that I deserve to be that woman. I'm not sure that

I can live up to what it would take to be her. So maybe I do belong on the street, always hiding from the likes of Big Jon, always wary of the next trick if it's a face I haven't seen before. Maybe that's all I'm worth, all I should ever look forward to. It would be an easier road, for sure, if on the surface it doesn't seem so rosy.

I'm not sure which road I will take though, but once I make this decision, one thing is for sure – that's it. It will affect the rest of my life. For better, or for worse. And I'm starting to think that making decisions might be another thing I'm no good at.

If you liked A Forgotten Tomorrow, you might like other titles in the Cutting Edge series.

The following is an extract from another Cutting Edge title. It's the first chapter of Thrill Seekers by Edwina Shaw.

CHAPTER 1

Three Days

Brian

Look. See that box? My dad's in there, in that box they're putting into the ground.

I can hear him scratching on the lid.

I want to scream and jump in after the clump of dirt they get me to throw, pull off the lid and rescue him. But my legs won't move and I stand like an empty tin man as the mud thuds on top of the shiny wood, muffling the sound of his fingernails tearing.

Two weeks ago Dad told us he was dying. Me and my little brother Douggie sitting there eating breakfast like it was any other day, Vegemite toast turning hard in my throat. Mum sucking the guts out of a cigarette and blowing it out towards the window, not looking at us.

'I'm not going to get better,' he said.

'Oh,' we said. 'Oh.'

What did he mean, I wondered. He'd been sick a long time, become skinny and bald and ugly, but people always got better. You got sick, you took your medicine no matter how bad it tasted, and then you were better. That's how it went.

'I'm going to die,' he said, then got up and left us sitting there.

'Mum?' I said. 'It's not true, is it?'

Douggie didn't say anything, just sat there with a half-chewed piece of Weetbix still in his open mouth, his eyes big and wide like a possum's in torchlight.

'Mum? He's joking right?'

Mum blew out the last of her smoke and ground the butt into her ashtray. 'Of course he's not joking, Brian,' she sighed. 'Your father's sick. Maybe you'd have realised if you weren't always off playing the fool with your friends on that bloody creek. Don't you notice anything that's going on around here? He's very sick. He's going to die.'

'I don't get it.'

'What's there to get? You're big enough to understand, to start pulling your weight around here.' She rubbed her forehead. 'You're going to have to be the man of the house soon. I can't do it on my own. I just can't.'

'You mean he's really going to die?'

'For God's sake, how plain do I have to make it?' She gulped the last of her tea. 'Yes. He's going to die. D.I.E.'

'You mean like Fluffy?' Douggie got it quicker than me. Our guinea pig had been mauled by the neighbour's red setter last winter and we'd had to bury the bits in a shoebox under the Poinciana tree.

'Like Fluffy.' Mum nodded to Douggie with a closed-lip smile.

He started to cry, even though he's only about a year younger than me, and Mum held him close and patted his hair.

'Sorry,' she said. 'I'm sorry boys. I don't know what we're going to do.' She glanced over like she expected me to cry too.

I didn't. I'm thirteen, way too big to cry. Anyway I didn't feel like crying. I was trying to figure it all out. It couldn't really be true. Guinea pigs, cats, dogs, people on TV, soldiers, they die. Not ordinary people like us. The nuns reckon Jesus died then came back to life again three days later. Old people, they die. Dads don't.

I couldn't eat anymore, it all tasted like the box we'd buried Fluffy in. I left Mum and Douggie holding on to each other at the table and went to my room, closed the door and lay on top of my unmade bed listening to the washing machine go round and round and round.

When I couldn't stand the whirring any longer, I got down on my knees and pointed my fingers to heaven like the nuns had taught me and promised to be good forever if only God would change His mind. I promised I'd never tease Douggie again, or pull his hair or make fun of the stupid way he talks. I'd make my bed and help Mum wash up and never talk back or sneak any more ciggies or money from her purse. I'd do all my homework and not throw rocks from the overpass. I wouldn't even think about touching girls' tits. I'd grow up and be a priest. I'd do that and never have any fun ever again, if that would make God change His mind. I made a deal, a bargain to save Dad's life. It felt like God was listening.

I made my bed straight away, tucked in the corners and folded down the sheet. I put on my school uniform and rubbed the mud off my sneakers with a bit of toilet paper wet with spit, gathered up the clothes from the floor and chucked them in the laundry. God was watching. I wasn't going to let Dad down.

'Come on Douggie, stop crying,' I said as I dragged him down the path to school. 'It's going to be all right. I've fixed everything.'

My teacher, Sister Bernadette, kept looking at me funny. She must have thought I was about to put pins on her chair again, because she couldn't seem to understand why I was being so good all of a sudden. At the end of the week she made me wear the best student Holy Medal home. That made Dad smile. But it didn't make him better.

He stopped going to work, which wasn't like Dad, and lay in bed all day coughing, with Mum and Gran and strange nurses fussing over him. When I tried to get him to laugh or play with the ball they said 'Hush' and 'Leave your father in peace'. So I took Douggie out to the backyard instead and we kicked the football to each other in silence. It wasn't fun anymore. It seemed like nothing was fun.

Every night I prayed hard, made more promises, told God I'd get Douggie to be a priest too if that would help. But as the days wore on and Dad got thinner and greyer and the stink in his room started to turn me away, I knew that God wasn't listening. Had never been listening. And that even Mother Mary in her long blue gown didn't see me, there on my knees, by my bed, crying.

The deal was off. I stole half a packet of Mum's Marlboros and headed down to the creek with my mates. Smoked up a storm.

The sun kept shining like always. I went to school every day and pretended I was normal. But it felt like I wasn't really me at all. The real me who used to laugh and tease and chase after the girls had disappeared, gone away camping. He'd left me, some sort of robot double, to keep on doing the stupid things I had to do every day.

It wasn't me.

On the day before Dad died I went in and sat beside him on the bed, trying not to look at the way his skull showed through the skin on his face and his bald head, the way the tube sticking out of his arm bulged up the skin. Tried to see Dad the way he used to be, before cancer turned him into something scary.

'Hey,' he said. His lips were cracked, white pasty stuff was sticking in the corners, and his breath smelled bad.

'Dad, I…um…' The words wouldn't come. I wanted to say, 'Please don't die. Don't go and leave me behind.' But I couldn't.

'Brian, listen to me.' He coughed and scrunched up his face. I handed him a tissue from the box on the bedside table that was crammed with pill bottles and a vase of flowers with brown edges and dirty water. 'You take care of your mother and your brother for me. Okay?'

I nodded.

'Be a good boy.' He coughed again and lay back on his pillows with his eyes closed, holding onto his belly.

'I will.'

He didn't say any more, just lay there breathing hard and raspy, a deep crease between his eyebrows.

'I love you Dad,' I whispered as I rested my head to his bony chest. I lifted his arm and put it, loose and floppy, around my shoulders. But I couldn't stay there long because of the stink that was coming from under the sheets. It smelt like the dump where we go hunting for treasures. Something rotten.

Mum came in and bustled me out. She didn't like us kids being in there bothering Dad. She looked almost as skinny as him and was smoking more than ever. I'd even seen her helping him to have a drag on her cigarette, putting the butt up to his crusted lips, brushing them with her fingertips, smoothing back where his hair should have been with her other hand.

The day he died they sent us to school like it was any other day. Pushed us into the bedroom and told us to kiss Dad goodbye. He was still sleeping. I bent down to kiss him on the lips. But they were so awful, so death-ugly, that I changed my mind and gave him a quick kiss on the forehead. I should've kissed him on the lips. I would have, if I'd known that goodbye was forever.

And so, sometime around lunchtime on Thursday, while I picked at a peanut paste sandwich and pretended to smile at some kid's stupid joke in the school yard, Dad died. Later, one of my aunties came and picked me up early from school. I knew as soon as I heard the school gate clanking that it had happened. I tried not to see Aunty Joan, willed it not to be her, even tried praying again, but she got nearer and nearer until she stood at the classroom door with her eyes swollen, twisting a man's hanky in her hands. She whispered to Sister in the doorway, dark evil figures against the afternoon sun. Sister kept glancing over at me with a frown, nodding and frowning some more.

Her sensible nun shoes tapped to the front of the classroom.

'Class,' she said. 'I have some bad news. Brian's father has died. He has to go home.'

I wanted to smash her wrinkly old nun face into the floorboards. She told. I hadn't told anyone, not even my best mate, Jacko. On purpose. I didn't want any of them to know. Not until I was ready. Till I'd figured it out. Till I could joke about it so they wouldn't look at me like I was some kind of freak, which is what they were doing now, their eyes and mouths gaping.

Aunty Joan came over and wrapped her arm around me. I shrugged it off, gathered my stuff and walked out without looking at anyone. I could never go back in there again.

That afternoon the sky turned black just like the bible said it did the day Jesus died. It cracked open with thunder and heavy rain and I stood in the middle of our street until my clothes were soaked, letting the rain hide my tears. Trying to feel real. To get clean again. But I couldn't clean my insides.

The house was full of aunties and uncles, all talking. There were cakes and biscuits, even some with chocolate, but I wasn't hungry. I didn't want treats. I wanted Dad back. And if I couldn't have that I wanted the house quiet, just me and Mum and Douggie, so I could think. So we could make a circle together and understand that our number had gone from four to three.

But Mum was surrounded by an army of grown ups who wouldn't let me near her, who kept pouring booze that smelt like Christmas pudding into her glass, lighting her cigarettes, telling me to shush and let my mother be. No one even noticed I was wet.

I couldn't see Douggie anywhere. Then I glimpsed him hiding under the kitchen table, curled into a ball sucking his thumb. Mum had made him stop doing that ages ago. I got down on my hands and knees on the lino and crawled between the wall of stockinged legs to join him. When I got close I heard him making a funny whimpering sound, like a dog that's been locked out.

'Douggie,' I whispered. 'Doug?'

He didn't take the thumb out of his mouth, but he looked at me. He looked so scared that it made me feel brave and I put my hand on his back and patted him a bit.

He uncurled then and came to me, tried to bury himself in my puny wet chest.

I'm going to have to look after him. But I don't know how.

Douggie's not here today. They said he was too upset to come, too young. Not me though. I'm thirteen. Old enough for a funeral. Old enough to look after everyone. Douggie, and Mum too.

So I can't jump in after Dad, no matter how much I want to.

Anyway, you never know what might happen. Remember Jesus? He died, but He wasn't really dead. So I'll wait.

I'll wait three days.

I waited three days; I've waited three bloody years. God sucks.

Bone Song
SHERRYL CLARK
Melissa is running scared . . . and she daren't make friends or tell anyone her secret.

Breaking Dawn
DONNA SHELTON
Is friendship forever? Secrets, betrayal, remorse and suicide.

Don't Even Think It
HELEN ORME
One family's terrible secret.

Ecstasy
A C FLANAGAN
Carrie's supposedly dutiful friend, Mae–Ling, is fighting for her life after an ecstasy overdose. But Mae–Ling is not the only one hiding dark secrets.

Gun Dog
PETER LANCETT
Does having a gun make you someone? Does it make you strong or does it actually make you weak? Stevie is about to find out.

Hanging in the Mist
PETER LANCETT
Living in a high–rise crumbling tower block, with parents more interested in crack than you, is no fun.

Marty's Diary
FRANCES CROSS
How do you cope as a teenager when step–parents enter your life.

MindF**k
FANIE VILJOEN
Three disaffected youths, a beautiful hitch–hiker, a mind–blowing rock concert and a descent into darkness.

Rans❖m

Life at the **CUTTING EDGE**
For more gritty reads in the same series

Seeing Red
PETER LANCETT
The pain and the pleasure of self–harm.

See You on the Backlot
THOMAS NEALEIGH
Tony is 'Clown Prince of the Sideshow'. He has carnival in his blood. But the fun and laughter stops backstage.

Scarred Lions
FANIE VILJOEN
A scarred, man–eating lion prowls the game reserve. Will Buyisiwe survive? And heal the wounds from the past?

Stained
JOANNE HICHENS
Crystal is a teenage mum in despair. Can't anyone see the tragedy unfolding? Her only hope is Grace next door.

The Finer Points of Becoming Machine
EMILY ANDREWS
Emma is a mess, like her suicide attempt, but everyone wants her to get better, don't they?

The Only Brother
CAIAS WARD
Sibling rivalry doesn't end at the grave – Andrew is still angry with his only brother; so angry he's hitting out at everyone, including his dad.

The Questions Within
TERESA SCHAEFFER
Scared to be different? Constance has always felt like an outcast.

Thrill Seekers
EDWINA SHAW
Douggie starts hearing voices and there's nothing Brian can do, as he watches his brother and his mates spiral out of control.

Rans✺m